COUNTESS NOBODY

COUNTESS NOBODY

LYNN KIELE BONASIA

EGMONT

USA

New York

EGMONT

We bring stories to life

First published by Egmont USA, 2011
443 Park Avenue South, Suite 806
New York, NY 10016

1 3 5 7 9 8 6 4 2

www.egmontusa.com
www.lynnkielebonasia.com

Library of Congress Cataloging-in-Publication Data
Bonasia, Lynn Kiele.
Countess nobody / Lynn Kiele Bonasia.
p. cm.
Summary: Fifteen-year-old Sophie, upset to learn that her twin brother Sam is a count but she has
no title, writes a blog about an imaginary count's exploits, which becomes so popular that it greatly
improves her visibility at school but creates problems that require a radical solution.
ISBN 978-1-60684-207-2 (pbk.) — ISBN 978-1-60684-251-5 (electronic book)
[1. Blogs—Fiction. 2. Fame—Fiction. 3. Brothers and sisters—Fiction. 4. Twins—Fiction.
5. High schools—Fiction. 6. Schools—Fiction. 7. Family life—Massachusetts—Fiction.
8. Massachusetts—Fiction.] I. Title.
PZ7.B63652Cou 2011   [Fic]—dc22   2011002493

Printed in the United States of America

CPSIA tracking label information:
Printed in April 2011 at Berryville Graphics, Berryville, Virginia

**FOR CATHERINE,
CHRISTIAN, AND ALEX.**
· ·

ACKNOWLEDGMENTS

• •

Many thanks to my agent, Molly Lyons, for helping me tap my inner fifteen-year-old and break into an exciting new genre. And thanks to Regina Griffin, Alison Weiss, and everyone at Egmont for their support.

Also, thank you to the wonderful real-life French family who inspired this story. *Vous serez toujours dans mon cœur!*

CHAPTER ONE

· ·

Usually, I love my brother. But sometimes, I wish he would vanish into the ether. This was one of those times. Somehow, I'd managed to control myself the entire school bus ride home. But the minute we stepped onto the sidewalk, Samuel Delorme encountered the wrath of Sophie.

"It's not fair, Sam!" I whipped around so fast my braid whacked me in the teeth. "Why would she pick *you* for the French team? You don't know a *cochon* from a *cornichon*."

Sam must've thought I was going to hit him. He ducked. "Pigs and pickles," he said. "And I'm almost as good as you."

Since when did *almost* count? *"C'est pourri!"* I said. I started walking fast, which drove him crazy. He could run circles around me, but I could walk so fast he couldn't keep up.

"What's that mean?" he asked. He jogged to catch up. "Sophie!"

"It means this is *rotten*. I wanted to go to Montreal. I had my heart set on it, and now you get to go. Story of my life." I let my backpack slide off my shoulder and caught it in my hand, then made a sharp turn onto the slate path that led to the front porch of our

Victorian, with its chipping paint and Halloween lights still strung up the posts. Did I mention it was April?

Sam took a couple more long strides to catch up. "Story of your *life*? Isn't that a bit melodramatic, sis?"

Melodramatic? After he got invited to Amy Van Horn's party and I didn't? After the Putnam High School cheerleaders collectively Tweeted that he had the best smile in the tenth grade? After he got asked to the senior prom, albeit by a girl who wanted to go as just friends? He still was going to get to go. There was no doubt Sam's star was on the rise while his poor twin seemed to be trapped in a black hole.

I climbed two porch steps so I'd be taller than him, then whipped around again, this time more successfully managing the trajectory of the incoming braid. "I may have come out of the womb first, but you seem to come out first in everything else." My ears felt hot.

"Lighten up, Soph," he said. He slid past me, went over to the porch chair, and checked under the cushion for the Easter candy he'd stashed there. He grabbed a couple of chocolate eggs and held one out to me. I ignored the peace offering.

I turned and stomped up the stairs, opened the door, and threw my backpack onto the floor.

Sam threw his on top of mine. "And let's not talk about *wombs*, okay?"

I passed by the living room and headed straight for the kitchen, in search of the only thing that I knew would comfort me: my dad's forever-on-sale generic Oreos. Hey, things were tight, and in the end, cookies were cookies.

"Mom!" I heard Sam say from the hallway.

"Hey, Samuel," she said.

"Hi, son," Dad added.

I ran for the living room. How had I managed to miss them both? This couldn't be good. The last time I'd come home from school and found Mom at the house during Dad's week, it was because our cat Calvados, Calvo for short, had been hit by a UPS truck. (Which he survived, despite the fact that all his internal organs had ended up in his hind leg. A hernia, the vet had called it. But there was no way he could survive another ordeal like that, not even if he had eight lives left.)

I sprinted into the living room and hip-checked Sam out of the way. "Mom, what are you doing here?" She looked like she had come straight from work, where she was a media planner for a big ad agency. She was still wearing her gray business suit with her pearls. "Is it Calvo?"

She leaned in and kissed me on the forehead. "Calvo is fine, honey. Your dad and I just had something we wanted to discuss with you guys."

"Hey, Soph," Dad said. He looked nervous. Mom had that effect on him even four years after the divorce.

"So which one of you is coming out of the closet?" I asked.

Mom raised her eyebrows. Dad coughed. Sam howled.

"Good one," he said. I liked my twin again.

"Enough, you two." Mom was trying to hold back a smile.

"Sit." Dad pointed to the love seat.

This was all too weird. It felt like a bad Lifetime movie. Kids come home. The parents sit them down. All that can be heard is the *tick, tick* from the clock on the mantel. Words are spoken. Suddenly, the world shifts, things explode. Nothing is ever the same. *Kids, your dad and I are splitting.*

Well, frankly—thank goodness—I had managed to block out the details surrounding that grand proclamation. You'd think a couple of products of divorce like Sam and me might like seeing their parents together. No way. Mom turned into a robot when she was around Dad. She became stiff and rattled off the same tired phrases: *Hal, when are you going to take down those Halloween lights? Your check was late again. What do you have the thermostat set to? It's freezing in here. The Esses will catch their death.* (Our collective name since birth: the Esses. Samuel and Sophie. Better than Thing One and Thing Two, I suppose.)

As for Dad, a college physics professor who spent his days flexing his *smart* muscle, he just got monosyllabic. *Sure. Yes. Sorry.*

And then there always was the elephant in the room, who didn't happen to be particularly elephantine, nor was she actually in the room at this moment. Dad and his girlfriend, Taylor, had been going out for almost three years and yet he still did everything he could to hide her existence from Mom. If he knew Mom was coming, he'd shove Taylor's food processor into the cupboard. He'd run through the house and make sure none of her earrings were lying around—Taylor was notorious for leaving her jewelry in random places. (Had it been less earthy-crunchy, I might have been tempted to borrow it.) One time, I'd even caught him taking her pink razor out of the shower. As if Mom would even check the shower. And if she did, wouldn't she just assume the razor belonged to me? After all, I'd been shaving my legs for at least four years (two before it was actually necessary). Of course, despite Dad's best efforts, Mom knew about Taylor. They'd even seen each other once or twice. I don't think Mom was bothered by Taylor or the idea of Dad having a girl-friend. After all, Mom was the one who'd bailed on the marriage in the first place. I just think that, for whatever reason, Dad felt like he was cheating on his wife. Maybe he never got over Mom. Maybe all kids want to think that about their separated parents.

Sam sprawled on the love seat by the fireplace. Mom and Dad sat at far ends of the couch. All that was left for me was the space on the cushion between them, the broken rocking chair, or the floor. I wasn't feeling the energy on the couch and opted for the threadbare Oriental. Calvo came over and rubbed along my thigh, leaving gray hairs on my black tights. I scratched him behind the ears.

"Can I get a cookie?" I asked.

"In a minute," Mom said. "I brought you some fresh-baked choc-olate chips. They're on the counter."

Sweet. Though, I didn't want to make Dad feel like his cookies were inadequate, so I just uttered a subdued "Thanks." After all, this was his week. I'd always believed we should be nicer to the parent whose week it was.

There was the *tick, tick* of Grandma's old clock on the mantel, right on cue. My stomach growled. Calvo rattled off a comforting purr.

"Hal!" Mom finally yelled.

Dad jumped a little, then leaned forward. "In fewer than six weeks, you're going to be sixteen."

"Time flies, doesn't it, Soph?" Sam tossed a pillow at my head and missed. "Seems like yesterday I was biting your butt in the bathtub."

"You're gross," I said.

Dad fidgeted in his seat. He tugged on the neck of his T-shirt. The little vein at his temple pulsed. "There are some things about the family you're old enough to know now. Your mom and I had always agreed to tell you before your sixteenth birthday. So here we are."

"Is this the sex talk?" *Oh, God, please not that suicide-provoking conversation again.* "We already had the sex talk, don't you remember?" I pleaded.

"No, Soph," Sam cut in. "He said it was about the family. Maybe we're about to find out we come from a long line of outlaws. Serial killers."

"Maybe we have the Alzheimer's gene," I said.

Mom scowled. "Sophie!"

Sam continued. "Or maybe our ancestors were slaveholders."

"Samuel!" Dad scolded.

"Pirates?" I asked.

Sam brought all his fingertips to one point and rocked his wrists. "Maybe we're in the mob," he said with a lame Italian accent.

"We're French, you doofus."

"And German," Mom added.

"And you both just happen to descend from a long line of French noblemen," Dad said.

Sam un-sprawled. Mom sighed. I shot up to my knees.

"Remember how I told you I used to spend my summers in Normandy when I was a little kid?" Dad started again.

"You did?" Sam asked. *Of course* he did. How could Sam not remember a thing like that? *Hello . . . Normandy?*

"And I showed you pictures of my *grand-mère*'s château?"

For the first time, I noticed a framed picture resting on the coffee table, along with some old letters and a small carved wood box. I remembered him showing us the photo, though even I had never given it much thought: foreign country, big old house, dead French grandmother we'd never met.

"French noblemen. What does that mean, exactly?" Sam asked.

"*La noblesse,*" I said. I didn't know either but it sounded elegant.

"It just means I—*we*—descend from a long line of people who are privileged," Dad said.

Mom cleared her throat.

"I don't mean privileged as in better than anyone else. I just mean it's a tradition that goes back to the Middle Ages—to feudal times. One of our ancestors was appointed by King Louis XI, and then his title was carried down from generation to generation."

This was sort of like finding out you're a princess. Like that movie *The Princess Diaries*. I was savoring every moment. "Title?" I asked.

"Does this mean we're rich?" Sam asked. He had that crazy look in his eye, like when he gets too close to Michelle Alberghetti or a plate of mashed potatoes.

Mom let out a guffaw. I scowled at her. I assumed she was just jealous because she wasn't part of *la noblesse*. In fact, she came from a family of German hatmakers. *Très romantique*. Not.

"I wish," Dad said. He sighed and leaned back into the cushion. "As with most of the French nobility these days, the money is gone. Most of it went into trying to keep up their ridiculously large decaying old homes."

"Châteaux," I corrected.

"After *Grand-mère* passed, the house had to be sold to pay the back taxes. Each family member ended up with a few euros. That's basically it."

Sam slumped back into the love seat. "So then, what's the point?"

"You said something about a title," I reminded him.

Mom winced.

"Well. I guess I'm sort of a count," Dad said.

Sam and I looked at him. Sam started laughing. "Sophie, you remember the Count on *Sesame Street*? 'I like to count. . . . *One* ah-ha-ha. *Two* ah-ha-ha . . .'"

"Forget him. Think Dracula." Maybe I should have actually read those *Twilight* books my best friend, Kimmy, had given me. "Sam! We might be vampires!"

"Sophie." Mom sighed and shook her head.

"For the most part, it's just an empty title," Dad continued. "Back in the day, it might have gotten you the right to hunt or avoid paying certain tariffs. Maybe boss around some vassals. They'd let you wear a sword. And you got one of these." Dad opened the wood box. Sam and I leaned in.

"What is it?" Sam asked.

"A coat of arms."

It was a big gold ring with a crest, a rectangle that curved to a point at the bottom, etched into its flat oval face. Within the crest were four squares. On the top left and the bottom right was the same image of a five-petal flower. The other two diagonal squares depicted ships. There was another square in the middle—overlapping the other four—which contained three fleur-de-lis. *Three* fleur-de-lis for the three nobles: Sam, Dad, and me. I knew that wasn't the original intention, but I could let myself think that. The ring was pretty cool. I wondered how it might look on my finger, or on a chain around my neck. Maybe when I turned eighteen, I'd get the symbol tattooed on my back or my ankle. Then again, maybe not.

Suddenly, it occurred to me we had a problem. There were two of us and only one ring—not that I expected Dad to be kicking it anytime soon. But all our lives, it had always been about "one each" for us. We'd always split everything right smack down the middle, which was probably the only reason we hadn't killed each other yet. And even then, it always seemed like Sam got the bigger half. "So, who gets the r——" I said.

"So, if you're a count, what's Papa?" Sam interrupted.

"*Hello*, I was asking a question here." I glared at my annoying brother.

Dad ignored me and picked up an old envelope with a fancy seal on it. He slipped out what looked like an invitation, then smiled with an unmistakable upwelling of pride. "Your grandfather is a marquis. In fact, when he and *Maman* got married, they held a wedding with over five hundred guests at the *Hôtel des Invalides* in Paris. From what I hear, it was quite a ceremony."

"Are there pictures?" I asked.

"Tons," Mom groaned, as if she'd been exhausted by them at one point or another. Or she was just being jealous again. She and Dad got married by a justice of the peace in the Cambridge courthouse.

"How come you never showed us?" Sam asked.

"Like I said, we were just waiting for you to be old enough. We didn't want you thinking this made you special. I mean, it *is* special, and *you* are, but, you know, kids sometimes blow things out of proportion."

"So if Papa is a marquis, will you take his title when he dies?" Talk about out of proportion. Sam was already killing off relatives.

"I doubt it. Your uncles Claude and Bert would have to die first. I'm third in line," Dad explained.

"Like poor Prince Harry," I said. This new aristocracy business might actually give me a shot with the royals.

"It does work a bit like British royalty," Dad said.

"Without the family jewels," Mom sniped.

"So your brothers, what are they now?" Sam was grilling Dad.

"They're counts."

"And what am I?" Sam asked.

"You're a count, too," Dad said.

And that was when it hit me. The most remarkable thing. The air rushed from my lungs. I squeezed my eyes shut and crossed both hands at my chest, something I might have picked up from an elf scene in *The Lord of the Rings*, I don't remember. I took a deep breath and bowed my head.

"And *I* am a count*ess*," I said, with gravitas and an emphasis on the *ess*. Wasn't life simply remarkable? Wasn't it amazing how fast things could change? One minute I could be lamenting a lost trip to Montreal. And the next, I could be a countess. With this revelation, my whole future seemed to unfurl before me. I would attend college in Paris, then move to Normandy, live as an expatriate, and take up the cause célèbre of the homeless aristocracy. I'd amass a small army of displaced nobility, innkeepers, and old ladies with cats. We'd become the talk of Paris, banding together to raise enough funds to buy back our castles and live happily ever after, gathering for *croque monsieur* and fine Armagnac, smoking Gauloises, and sharing our favorite passages of Colette. (I hadn't read Colette but I'd heard she was a bit racy, so naturally, I was curious.) And it would be at one of these gatherings that I'd meet the love of my life, a wealthy *dûc*, perhaps. . . .

It occurred to me I'd been daydreaming for quite a while, yet no one had spoken. I looked up.

Mom's brows were scrunched and she was shaking her head at Sam, who seemed confused. Dad was stuffing the wedding invitation back into its envelope. He looked grim.

"What is it?" I asked.

"Tell her, Hal," Mom insisted.

"Ellen, please." Dad slid his palms down his twill slacks, a look of panic in his eyes, like a cow going to slaughter. "Well, see, the thing is . . . This title we're talking about? It's only passed down to the males in the family," Dad said.

Sam looked at me; then he snatched the box with the ring. "Cool."

I could feel my face heat up.

"You're still part of the family. I mean, it's still in your blood. It's just not the way the actual title is passed." Dad ran his hand over his face. "Look, it's a stupid rule. I'm sorry, hon—"

Mom had kept her peace long enough. "Honestly, Sophie. What do you care about some stuffy old title? I mean, what difference does it make? I've dreaded this moment from the day you were born. We've always tried to treat you two exactly the same, to give you the same experiences and opportunities. There's nothing fair about it. But there's nothing we can do about it, either. I've lived my whole life without a title and I've done just fine." If only my ears had been able to absorb her words. But all I was picking up was static. "And, Sam, I want you to be sensitive to your sister."

"Aw, heck, I didn't mean anything by it." He closed the box and set it back on the coffee table.

"I'm going upstairs." I stood up fast, not realizing that Calvo had been nestled against my back. He shot across the room. I brushed the cat hair from my legs. I wasn't going to give them the satisfaction of seeing how destroyed I truly was.

"Come on, Soph," Dad said.

"I'll come up with you." Mom rose from the couch.

"No, *really*. I'm fine. I just need some time." I felt my nose twitch, signaling the forthcoming deluge of tears. What would a countess do? How would a countess behave in this situation? What difference did it make? I fled the room and ran up the stairs.

"She'll cool off. Just leave her alone," I heard Sam say as I rounded the top of the staircase.

No, I would not cool off! Not ever! Like the ring, my destiny had slipped through my fingers. Even worse, I'd just learned I descended from a long line of self-important male chauvinist pigs. Here we were, two children with the same set of parents, identical lineage, having emerged nearly simultaneously from the same womb. Yet one would go on to a charmed life while the other was destined for banal mediocrity.

CHAPTER TWO

● ●

Banal mediocrity didn't sit particularly well with me. After skip-
ping dinner and eventually crying myself to sleep, I woke up in the
middle of the night. Teenage insomniac that I am, I got up to roam
the house, which was something I often did. I always liked how
darkness changed things, softened them. I opened my bedroom
door. Moonlight flooded through the hall window and made white
rectangles on the wood floor. I stepped into the nearest one, hoping
it might offer up some magic clarity.

All I got was Dad's soft snore coming from his bedroom across
the hall.

In my pajamas, bathrobe, and slippers, I padded down the stairs
and into the kitchen. By now, I knew which steps and floorboards
would be most likely to rat me out with their creaks, so I avoided
them. On the kitchen counter sat the bag of chocolate chip cookies
Mom had left. I was surprised to see that Sam hadn't touched them.
Perhaps counts didn't eat chocolate chip cookies. I tore into the bag
and stuffed an entire cookie into my mouth, not chewing, allowing
my saliva to melt away the dough around the chocolate. Counts and

countesses ate artisan bread, Brie, and dark chocolate. Commoners sucked the life out of chocolate chip cookies.

Dad had left the dishes in the drainboard without drying them. Something inside was catching the light, throwing a blue reflection onto the floor. I moved closer and saw that it was the fancy butter knife we'd been given by our neighbor, the cat lady, last Christmas. It was silver with a handle that was bejeweled with colored glass stones. I remembered thinking how beautiful it was when Dad unwrapped the gift. Now I pulled it from the utensil bin and held it in my hand, liking how the smooth stones pressed into the skin of my palm. After another cookie, I went back upstairs and took the knife with me.

From the top of the stairs, I noticed Sam's door was ajar. When he was younger, he had always been afraid of monsters, specifically a one-eyed ogre named Finster who lived under his bed. Every night he would leave the door open, hoping it would leave. Or maybe Sam just wanted Dad and me to hear his screams. Sam could be such a wimp sometimes. If this was to be his legacy, no wonder French nobility was facing extinction.

Dad snorted and I jumped. The movement set me on the path toward Sam's room. Back when we were kids, we used to go into each other's rooms all the time. But that stopped when we hit middle school and we both became aware of the body parts the other didn't have.

I pushed through the door. There was enough moonlight for me to navigate through Sam's dirty T-shirts, sweatshirts, and jeans on the floor without breaking my neck. The room smelled like feet, which was pretty much the way it always smelled unless overpowered by the stench of B.O. Let's face it. Boys are gross, with the exception of Spencer Kavanaugh, lacrosse star and captain of the math team—athletic and mathy, a devastating combination. I was willing to bet his room didn't smell like feet. But Spencer and me, that was a whole other story, one that hadn't been written yet.

I approached my brother's bed, made eye contact with the stuffed monkey in the corner, and felt guilty. What was I doing, spying on my brother? None of this was his fault.

Sam was tangled up in the covers, with a bare arm and leg splayed across the mattress. I had always been the kind of kid who stayed tucked in the covers all night, while Sam always looked like he'd been dropped onto the bed from the third story of a building.

I inched my way forward until I arrived at the edge of the mattress. What was it about Sam that all the girls at school liked so much? What made him more popular than me? I guess he was okay-looking, and to his credit, he didn't seem to know it. He had a full head of blond hair that, unlike mine, had body and always looked like it was moving, even when he wasn't. He wasn't a big kid, but he was strong and lean. We both were. He'd been on the swim team since sixth grade and I ran track.

Sam faced the window. Just as I leaned in to get a better look at his face, he rolled over. I froze and caught my breath. It was the twin thing. The Esses. We had this sixth sense about each other, like I always knew when he was in the room. I could sense it. He must've been sensing me now.

I always thought he looked more like me when he was sleeping. For one thing, our eyes are different colors, which you can't tell when they're closed. Mine are blue, while his are brown. And when we're awake, my face is usually screwed up with expression, while his is usually smooth and blank. A good poker face, Dad always said about him. About me, Mom always said with the faces I make, I should start banking the Botox now.

I stared at my brother's jaw, which seemed much more angular than I remembered. I examined his nose, how long and straight it was. It looked like a royal nose. Mine was stumpy and upturned. Until that very moment, I'd never minded having Samuel as my twin brother. Somehow, after today, all that had changed. A shiver shot through me and I tightened my fists. I felt the bumps in the knife handle and realized I was still holding it. Why in the world was it in my hand? Had I subliminally brought it upstairs to act out some Shakespearean tragedy? Sister slays brother in jealous fury over his title. Because as far as I could tell, there was no bread in need of buttering up here on the second floor.

"Sophie?" Sam said.

I jumped. "Sam."

"What are you doing?" he asked, his voice full of sleep.

"Nothing, I was just—I couldn't sleep." I slipped the knife into my pajama bottoms. It was cold.

Sam pulled himself up to an almost-sitting position. "Hey, look. I feel bad about today."

I slid to the foot of his bed, where he wouldn't be able to see my face clearly enough to know that I'd been crying. I picked up the corner of his Patriots blanket and started peeling off the appliqué logo.

He continued. "Really. I mean it. I know it's not fair. We've always shared everything. We should be able to share this, too."

"Yup, well . . . that isn't happening." I felt that twinge at the back of my nose. Remarkable things, tear glands, and how productive they could be.

"Besides, it's just a stupid title," Sam said. "It means nothing."

Then why did it seem to mean everything to me? It probably didn't take a shrink to figure that out. What habitually invisible teenage girl wouldn't love something to distinguish her from everyone else? And no, not the latest Coach bag or bejeweled Juicy sweat suit, though I'd be the first to admit it would be nice if we could afford fancy things like that once in a while. But this was something altogether different. Something real and ancient that all the money in the world couldn't buy. A birthright. It was something no one else could have. No one. Not even me. Just my stupid brother, my father, and my dumb uncles.

"Be honest," I said. "You have to be a little excited to be a count."

Sam yawned. "I don't even know what a count is. What counts have I known? Count Chocula. Which I don't even like, for the record."

I sat down on the bed. The knife . . . well, let's just say I was a tad uncomfortable. "I don't really know what it is, either. But I like how it sounds. And for those few minutes I thought I might be a countess, I was pretty pumped. I felt special." All hail Countess Nobody.

"I'd be more pumped if there was some cash involved." He rolled over.

I picked up his pillow and smacked him on the head with it. "Don't you dare diminish what this is. Whatever *this* is. It means something to our family. It obviously means something to Dad. Did you see how he lit up when he saw that invitation?"

"He hadn't even been born yet."

"I know. But he's grown up with this all his life," I said. "Good thing he had no sisters," I added.

"He must feel like crap. That's why they made such a big production out of today. And did you see Mom? She was so over it."

I looked down at Sam's ugly football bedspread, made uglier by my shredding. "I know you're just downplaying this whole thing to make me feel better."

I stood up. The knife slipped through my pants and fell onto the floor and, as luck would have it, landed on a metal belt buckle. *Ping!*

"What the heck was that?" Sam bolted upright. He reached over to the bedside table and turned on the light.

Think, Sophie. "It's nothing. I just brought the butter knife upstairs with me by accident." This was bad. "I wasn't . . . I honestly have no idea why."

He looked at me like I was a little crazy. Then he nodded and smiled.

"What?"

"The jewels on the handle," he said. "Remember? For our fourth or fifth birthday, Mom and Dad gave us crowns and scepters from some Disney flick. The handle looked just like that, with all these big plastic inlaid stones. You slept with the thing for a year."

"I did not."

Sam laughed.

"Shhhh!" I said, almost louder than his laugh. "You'll wake up Dad."

"I can't believe you don't remember that. It finally snapped in two and Mom tossed it. She said the edges were too sharp. You were inconsolable."

Had I always had some deep-seated obsession with aristocracy? Some eerie intuition about the family position? Some cellular memory? Might that explain my profound depression now?

"Go back to your room and try to get some sleep, will ya?" Sam said. He slipped back down beneath the covers. "All this will seem less tragic when the alarm goes off." He rolled toward the window. "And take the butter knife with you . . . and for the love of God, don't forget to wash it before you put it back!"

The next day at the bus stop, Sam and I agreed that we wouldn't mention any of this to our friends. If they knew he was a count, the girls who already pestered Sam would be pestering him even more. As for me, the fact that I was nothing would just add to my general nothingness. Good old invisible Soph. And even worse, kids might pity me. I didn't tell anyone, not even my best friend, Kimmy Strauss, who I'd known since third grade and who knew all my deepest, darkest secrets, including my obsession with Spencer Kavanaugh.

The next few days, Mom kept checking up on me ad nauseam. And Dad was almost as bad. I could see the weight of the world on his shoulders as he carried the pain his family had brought down on his only daughter. Of course, it wasn't his fault. I knew that. But I couldn't help snubbing him a little when we encountered each other in the kitchen. Like when I went in for a fake Oreo while he was standing right there, and then changed direction and went for one of Mom's cookies, which all week long, no one had touched but me, as if there'd been a sign on the bag that said SOPHIE. It was almost as if the cookies had been granted to me exclusively in exchange for the title of countess. A consolation prize.

The rest of the week, I found myself watching Sam more closely, too, just to see if this new knowledge changed him at all. I thought I detected an extra spring in his step as he passed Michelle Alberghetti in the halls, but I could have just been imagining that. If anything, he was being nicer to me.

I, on the other hand, wanted nothing more than to curl into a ball on my bed. I didn't have much of an appetite. Schoolwork started piling up. I wasn't even interested in my favorite TV show, the one where this chef guy travels all around the world and eats crazy things like beating frog hearts, grasshoppers, and hundred-year-old eggs. In fact, I was actually looking forward to going to Mom's condo Sunday, even though I'd always liked staying at Dad's better because that was the house we'd grown up in. Now the house seemed different. I felt like I didn't belong. At dinner, Dad tried to strike up a conversation, but I wasn't much in the mood for talking. And Sam tried to get me to play cards, and actually invited me to go to the mall, but I wasn't feeling it.

Even I couldn't really understand why I'd taken the news so hard. I mean, I'd been a perfectly happy person before all this had happened. Just a well-adjusted, slightly invisible teen, which probably wasn't the worst thing to be if you considered the pressure on the high-profile kids. They had images to live up to. The popular girls, who had to have perfect highlights, the latest handbags, and the jeans *everyone* was wearing. The jocks, who had to sweat their brains out in the gym every day. The smart kids, who practically had panic attacks if they brought home an A-minus. The stoners, who had to work hard not to pass out on their remedial math notebooks. And the troublemakers, who you heard about every Monday for having done something insane at each Saturday night's jock party (which Sam now regularly got invited to), always having to up the ante the next week.

No, besides the occasional bouts of jealousy over my brother's social successes, my life to this point had been simple and I liked it that way. My parents were divorced, though amicable, which wasn't unusual at Putnam High. I ran track. I did well in school. I got along okay with my brother. People seemed to like me in general. It could have been worse. But now, suddenly, I was miserable. Was it just that Sam had something I didn't? Something that probably would have meant a lot more to me than it did to him? (Like that trip to Montreal.) I was jealous. And maybe even a little bitter. I wasn't proud of that. But there seemed no point in denying it, either.

As the school bus rumbled to a stop on Friday, I saw Dad's girl-friend sitting on the steps of our house. It was a beautiful day and the daffodils Mom had planted years ago had started pushing their green fingers up through the soil. It always amazed me how things in nature could happen so fast. One day, you'd go to school and there'd be no leaves on the trees. You'd come home and the tree would have knuckles, swollen buds that had appeared out of nowhere, that were on the verge of bursting open. I always notice things like that. I'm not sure most people do.

Speaking of Mom, as I approached, I noticed that Taylor had her maroon sweatshirt folded on her lap, and there was a coffee grinder next to her on the step. She was gnawing on a stick of beef jerky, her secret addiction.

"Mom coming over?" I asked.

"How'd you guess?" she said. She peeled the wrapper down the shriveled brown wand and tore another chunk off with her molars. How a person could eat those things was beyond me.

Taylor's hair looked darker. She was always changing the color, only unlike the divas at school, she tended to make it lighter in the winter and darker in the summer. I'd once asked her why, and all she'd said was "balance." Taylor was into yoga, which kept her in great shape, though I could never figure out how beef jerky fit into the body-as-a-temple concept.

"Come sit for a minute," she said. She tapped the step.

I was in no hurry to start packing up my stuff to get ready to go to Mom's.

"Doesn't it bug you?" I asked. "How he hides all your stuff whenever she comes around, like you don't even exist?"

Taylor laughed. Her eyes crinkled up. She had a deep-throated laugh, like someone bigger, a guy even.

"I try not to let it bother me. I know he loves me," she answered. A breeze blew the beef jerky smell in my direction. I fanned it away. "Sorry," she said. She wrapped up what was left of the jerky and stuffed it under the coffee grinder lid. "I guess I'm hoping he'll come around eventually. Some men take longer than others to get over things."

"Four *years*?" I said.

"To you, that seems like a lifetime, I know," Taylor said. "But listen. I'm pretty sure your dad is happy to have me around." She picked up the grinder. "If this is the worst thing he does, I can handle it." She set it back down next to her. "For now."

"But don't you want to marry him someday? At the rate he's going, he'll be sixty by the time he's over it."

"You don't need to worry about it," she said. She pulled her hair back into a ponytail with an elastic that had been on her wrist. "So your dad told me about the French stuff. I'm sorry."

I hadn't seen that coming. "No big deal."

"It's a big deal if it means something to you," Taylor said. "Personally, I think it's silly in this day and age. It's elitist."

"Did you know about it?"

"He told me he was a count when we first started dating. I guess I'm being a hypocrite. At the time I think I was a little impressed." She laughed. "At the very least, maybe it'll help Sam with women."

"As if he needs it," I mumbled.

Taylor acted like she didn't hear. "Fortunately, *you'll* never need any help with the opposite sex."

"Please." I picked up a pebble and threw it at the neighbor's split-rail fence.

"I'm serious," she said. "You're getting more gorgeous every day."

I looked down at my skinny body. My concave chest. My bony knees, which I had to put a pillow between when I slept on my side so they wouldn't press into each other. "You're getting more near-sighted." I smiled. "But thanks."

Taylor blew a stray hair from her forehead. She was pretty, her-self, mostly when she didn't overdo the makeup. She had the most amazing ice-blue eyes, like you could see right into her. Sam said she must be made of glaciers, back when we were trying to find things wrong with her. Like all children of divorce wishing their parents would get back together, we had given Taylor the requi-site cold shoulder when she came on the scene. But she took it all in stride, and it wasn't long before we realized we actually liked having her around. She was different from Mom—less driven. Less busy. Taylor was type B, or even C, and proud of it. I liked that about her.

As I was contemplating Taylor's compliment and whether it was truly possible that I might be getting less ugly, a blue sedan sped around the corner. I recognized it right away. My instinct was to duck. But there was nowhere to hide, so I just sat there and watched as the love of my life (unbeknownst to him, of course) drove past. There were two other people in the car, and as they got closer, I could see the girls. One was a year older than me. I didn't know her name, but she was a cheerleader—in every sense of the word. I didn't recognize the other girl.

In that split second, it occurred to me that even high school had its own landed gentry, the lords and ladies, dukes and duchesses, counts and countesses, whose only birthrights were merely fortuitous genetics. Which I guessed was the same for the actual descendents of nobility—the males, at any rate. Life was a giant crapshoot.

Spencer must have recognized me. Or, more likely, thought I was someone else. He raised his hand and waved. The dark-haired girl in the backseat snapped her head around to see who'd stolen his attention. My face grew hot. The next instant, they were gone.

"Who was *that*?" Taylor asked. Her voice was annoyingly creamy.

"The crown prince of Putnam High, heir to the female student body," I sniped.

"Good one," Taylor said. "He waved, you know. Did you see?"

"Ugh." I wanted to crawl under the porch and die next to the squirrel whose skeleton Sam and I had found there when we were ten.

"You *did* see." Taylor winked. "Okay, I'll let it go." She fished in her pocket for what I hoped wasn't another stick of beef jerky. She produced a box of mints. "I just want to tell you a quick story. I think it might help." She took one and offered the box to me.

I grabbed a mint and popped it into my mouth. "Thanks."

"When I was about your age, I had this great-aunt who was very wealthy. She was about a million years old, and for some reason, she liked me. I think she saw something in me that reminded her of herself. And I liked her, too, not because she was rich. Probably in spite of it, seeing as everyone in the family seemed to be vying for a chunk of her money." The sun was getting lower in the sky. Taylor put her hand up to shield her eyes. "Every Tuesday after school I went over to her house, which was ridiculously cluttered with furniture, and I just hung out with her. Sometimes we went through her closet and she showed me her old dresses and shoes. Other times, when she wasn't feeling so well, we just sat around and played Scrabble. She'd give me a glass of sherry but made me promise not to tell my mother.

"Anyway, we became pretty close. One day when I went over, I could tell she wasn't feeling so hot. I made her some tea and she just sat in her chair. We didn't talk much. When she finally spoke, it was to tell me that she was going to leave me a 'large sum of money,' enough to pay for my college education, and then some. I told her she didn't have to do that, but she insisted. I'll never forget: when I left that day, I went to give her a kiss on the forehead like I always did and she reached up with her arthritic hand and held my face for a moment." Taylor stared at the ground. "I loved that old broad." She paused. "I never saw her again. She died the following Monday."

"She didn't leave you the money, did she?" I asked just to be polite. I wasn't an idiot. I could see where this was going.

"No. She either forgot or someone in the family intervened. Most of her estate went to my uncle and his kids. I was crushed. At the time, I took it pretty hard. I couldn't understand. I felt like she didn't love me after all."

"Maybe she just forgot because she was too sick," I offered.

"I'm sure of it. She was just an old, lonely woman who everyone kowtowed to because she had money. But it had never been about that for me." Taylor brushed some cat hair off her pants. "Of course she loved me."

"Okay, so I get it. You thought you had a fortune coming your way and in a moment, it was snatched away."

"The reason I'm telling you this story is not because of the fortune. It's because I had a really rough time with this for a while. I felt let down, not just by my great-aunt, but by my whole family." Taylor looked at me with her fierce blue eyes. I felt a chill. "It's not the same as your situation, but there are some similarities. Lots of 'if only's and 'what if's."

"I guess," I said. I pulled a thread from the fraying hem of my jeans.

"And one of the ways I got through the hurt was by writing about it."

I looked up at her. She didn't strike me as the writer type.

"Sophie, I've always thought you have a talent for observing things. So do your English teachers. You're a writer, Sophie. And when bad things happen in our lives, or even when they don't, writers write about it. We keep journals. It's how we work through stuff. You should try it."

All of a sudden, I was like, *Who* are *you?* Taylor, a writer? Wait until Sam got a load of this. "Do you still write?"

"I publish short stories here and there. And I've been working on a book of them for a few years now."

"Does Dad know?" I asked.

"I don't talk about it much. It's just a hobby," she said, and looked at her watch. "I have a class in twenty minutes. I should go." She started gathering up her stuff.

Taylor sometimes taught yoga to chair-bound seniors at the YMCA. Sam and I always wondered how she kept a straight face. I had to admit, knowing she was a writer now made me see her a little differently.

"Thanks for sharing, Taylor." I got up. "And good luck with that emotionally stunted father of mine."

Taylor laughed. "How did you two ever turn out so well adjusted?" she asked.

Well adjusted? I was glad somebody thought so. We hugged and she left.

Sunday night at Mom's, after we made our weekly transition, I decided to put Taylor's suggestion to the test. I sat down at my computer, cracked my knuckles, and opened a fresh Word document.

To whom it may concern at the French consulate:

My name is Sophie Delorme and I am an American-born daughter of a French count. I recently learned that my father's title will only be passed on to my twin brother. Surely you can understand my profound disappointment. In these modern times, doesn't it seem archaic to perpetuate such sexual inequality, particularly in such a progressive, forward-thinking country as France?

I am writing in the hopes that someone in your government might see the injustice and change the rule that prohibits noble titles to be passed down to female progeny. Here is an opportunity to lead the way for all of Europe, as you already have with cuisine, fashion, philosophy, and social reform. . . .

I had gotten that far when Mom came into my room with a batch of fresh-popped popcorn. Evidently, she had gotten it into her head I might conceivably eat my way out of the whole countess debacle. Somehow, I didn't think that was going to work, though I knew from the countless empty pints of Häagen-Dazs I'd found in the trash over the years that this was her own method of self-medication.

"Whatcha doing, Soph?" she asked. She set the bowl on the corner of my desk. I could smell the butter. "Did you catch up on your homework?"

I pushed away from the computer. "Take a look."

She leaned in and started reading. When she got to the end, she sighed. "Oh, Sophie." She had that familiar pained *mother* look on her face.

"What?" I asked. I refused to buy into her negativity. "I think it's eloquent, don't you? Though I was thinking maybe the letter might be more effective if it were in French. I could ask Madame Phippen to help—"

"I admire the effort, honey, but I honestly doubt you'll hear back. And I can't imagine anyone is going to change centuries-old French customs for some American kid."

I turned back to my desk. "You never know," I said. But I sort of did. I'd known all along. She was right.

"I think you should send it anyway, and see what happens. At least you're not just accepting things. You're doing something about it." Mom was a big-time doer. "Whatever the end result, you'll know you tried."

I shoved a handful of the popcorn into my mouth. It was still warm. "Thanks," I said.

Mom rubbed my back in circles like she used to when I was little.

"Actually, Taylor was the one who gave me the idea," I admitted.

There was an almost imperceptible break in Mom's circle rubbing.

"Taylor?" Mom said. "Really? How so?"

"I won't go into it, but she went through something similar as a kid and writing helped her."

"Writing?" She said it like maybe she was surprised Taylor knew how to read, let alone write. "You mean *letters*?"

"No, just writing. I was thinking I might start a journal or something."

"Funny. Your dad never told me Taylor liked to write." Mom grabbed for some popcorn.

"Mom, Dad hasn't even told you Taylor exists."

"True," she said with her mouth full.

"Besides, I think he doesn't really know much about it."

"Really?" she said. She swallowed. "Well, I think a journal would be a great idea, Soph."

Mom left, and I dug into the bowl of popcorn. A couple of minutes later, I heard the freezer door close. Mom was hitting the Häagen-Dazs.

CHAPTER THREE

· ·

Fathers, lock up your daughters. The French invasion is on. It's official. Count S has landed at Logan Airport and is taking the city of Boston by storm. Who is Count S, you ask? Just the tallest, smartest, most wealthy, handsome, and charming eligible European hottie to hit the states since Jude Law. We are so not kidding. Searing, mischievous brown eyes. Hair the color of espresso, and a long, straight nose that ends at a dashing white smile. And don't even get us started on his broad back and strong, tanned legs that, yes, we've had the privilege of seeing in workout shorts.

Did we mention Count S is a real, live French count? Move over, Prince Harry. We hear that S's father, known by his legions as Marquis de [something we can't share for fear we'll get our pants sued off], made his fortune developing real estate in Panama, which took him away from home for long stretches during the count's childhood. Rumor has it S grew up in an enormous château in the Loire Valley, raised by a pack of female wolves, otherwise known as his mother and aunts. As a child, he was homeschooled, and spent his summers at the family compound on the Riviera, where he cavorted with topless women who taught him everything he needed to know to garner his reputation as a French Casanova at the ripe age of nineteen. In fact, there are so many legends about his masculine prowess that, well, we'll have to feed them to you piecemeal for fear of spontaneously melting your hard drive.

Suffice it to say the count often travels with an entourage of women. Just this week he was spotted in a smokin' black Hummer with a couple of gorgeous ingénues by a young peasant who claims he waved to her. Get a grip, honey. What would a guy who's all that and a bag of chips be doing waving to a mere roadside commoner, unless she was hot herself, which we can unequivocally report is not the case.

But we digress. . . . Inside sources tell us that Count S will be attending a charity function in Boston this evening, and you can be sure we'll have our informants out in full force for an in-depth report, particularly to see what female accessories he'll be wearing. Stay tuned for details.

Adoringly, Mademoiselle Blogger

"Why are you making me go to this soup kitchen thing tonight?" Kimmy asked. "I've already logged in enough community service hours to graduate twice, and I'm only a sophomore."

Kimmy and I were on our way to the White Hen Pantry after school. She was having one of her Skittles cravings. It was a beautiful day and Sam had swim practice, so I figured instead of taking the bus, I'd catch a ride home with Mom when she came to pick him up.

"You mean the only reason you do something good in this world is to get credit for it?" I asked.

"Give me a break, Sophie," she said. Kimmy is shorter than I am, and has dark brown hair that falls around her face in loose waves. She has that fresh-scrubbed look, with pink cheeks and perfect dark eyebrows that arch in a way that makes her look wise, even if she isn't always. "I just told you how much I volunteer for stuff."

"Okay, honestly, I can't believe you haven't figured it out by now," I said. There were some blue flowers coming up by the fire hydrant. Hyacinth, I think. I caught their sweet fragrance.

"Figured out what?"

"The lacrosse team is sponsoring the soup kitchen. *Hello*."

"Spencer Kavanaugh." Kimmy rolled her eyes. "Last month it was the lacrosse team car wash. Only we don't have a car, so we had to pay Jimmy Tucker ten dollars to take us, and then another ten dollars to get his stupid car cleaned."

"I paid," I reminded Kimmy. "And it was worth every penny." Visions of Spencer, shirtless and soapy, the tan line from his lacrosse shirt that cut across his lower biceps, and how his hair kept falling into his eyes so he had to keep flicking it away, and when he did, his ab muscles rippled in an almost imperceptible way, except to the trained eye.

"Sophie." Kimmy was trying to get my attention but I wasn't ready to let go of the image. "Sophie!"

I was on the Spencer train. I wasn't getting off. "Did I tell you he waved at me from his car on Friday?"

"Get *out*." She moved her backpack, which looked like it weighed fifty pounds, from one shoulder to the other. "Maybe he was swatting at a fly."

"I swear! I have witnesses. Taylor saw."

"Maybe he thought you were someone else," Kimmy said. Not to be mean. I understood she was just being realistic.

"Yeah, that was my guess, too." I mean, seriously, why would a guy like Spencer be waving to me?

Kimmy let her backpack crash to the ground, then stretched her arms out to the sides. "And so we're going tonight just so you can share airspace with your über crush?"

"Basically." I kicked a stone and it skipped into the gutter.

"Okay." Kimmy slung the backpack over her shoulder again, and we continued on our Skittles mission. That was the thing about Kimmy. She was a good friend.

I slid on my pink cowl-neck sweater. Too dressy. I pulled it off and tossed it on the bed, then went back to the closet. What the heck did someone wear to work in a soup kitchen? My red long-sleeve henley? Too . . . red. For once I was actually intentionally trying to be innocuous. What about a T-shirt and a hoodie? Perfect. After all, part of my mission tonight was to be invisible. I wasn't just a volunteer. I was an informant.

Honestly, I'm not sure what had possessed me to start a blog about a made-up count, let alone a count named S. It didn't make much sense. Here I was, a thwarted countess, writing not about my brother, who was the actual count, but about a fictional version of a guy I had a mad crush on, who wasn't even French. I could have just started a journal, like Taylor suggested, but besides whining about my predicament, what did I really have to say? I thought it might be more fun to make something up, act out a little. Maybe this nobility stuff was all so elusive (and always would be) that I figured I might as well imagine what that life might have been like, but through the eyes of the only true royalty I knew, the popular high school kids, and the guy who, to me, epitomized aristocracy: Spencer Kavanaugh. Why did it really even have to make sense? All I know is that after I wrote that first entry, I felt better, like I'd set something in motion. I felt as if I'd chugged an energy drink (which I hate, because they taste nasty). But this . . . this was an altogether different kind of high.

And I felt even more validated when I saw that someone had actually read what I'd written. My first comment was from CELEBSTALKER19 in Brooklyn, NY.

> *How come I haven't heard of this fellow, darling? I know everyone who's anyone. I'm on the edge of my seat for more scoop.*

I had no choice but to oblige.

* * *

The room in the basement of the church smelled of must and garlic, and there were no windows. The only light came from the harsh overhead fluorescents. Let's just say even Kimmy, with her flawless skin, looked a little mottled and green, so you can imagine what the patrons of the place looked like.

Kimmy and I had gotten there early, before any of the lacrosse team even showed up, so they put us together to man the coffee and juice stations. There, we spent the night in the corner of the room, doling out plastic cups of red fruit punch to grown men and women like they were kindergarteners, though I seemed to mind it more than they did. Most of them were very grateful and friendly, and it sort of made me feel good to help, even if I had ulterior motives.

When the guys from the team showed up, some were assigned to the food station, where they spooned out globs of American chop suey onto yellow and green plastic plates, or dished out salad, bread, and brownies with metal tongs. The rest of the guys got to help with cleanup. As I'd expected, Spencer had shown up with one of the girls who had been in the car the other day, the brunette who'd been sitting in the backseat. Her name, Kimmy had found out, was Destiny. She might be someone's destiny, but I doubted very much that she was Spencer's. She laughed like a seal.

Destiny seemed to have no trouble serving food in a pink cash-mere belly shirt to a roomful of mostly middle-aged men. She and Spencer had been relegated to the brownie station. They wore matching hairnets and plastic gloves, partly because they had to, and partly, I suspected, because Destiny wanted Spencer and the rest of the lacrosse team to know that nothing, not even a piece of flesh-colored elasticized mesh, could diminish her corn-fed good looks.

Once again, Destiny's caterwaul pierced the air, rising above the din of metal utensils scraping over plastic plates.

"Isn't this painful for you?" Kimmy asked. She poured some cream into a cup and handed it to a man with sad eyes. "Why do you put yourself through this?"

"I don't know," I said. "It doesn't bother me so much, I guess." I wasn't paying attention and overpoured the juice so that anyone who went for that cup would end up berry-stained. "Somewhere in the back of my mind, I tell myself that he's having fun with these bimbos but, eventually, if he's the man of substance I believe him to be, he'll get bored with them and settle down with a sensible girl."

"Did someone slip something into your fruit punch? You really think you're going to land Spencer? In this lifetime?"

"Maybe not this lifetime," I said. "But I can wait."

I looked over and realized that what I'd thought had been Destiny laughing had actually been Destiny shrieking. One of the patrons, a woman with a limp who may have been a tad intoxicated, had tripped and splattered red sauce all over Destiny's sweater. Spencer ran to the kitchen and came back with a damp cloth. He handed it to Destiny.

"See that?" I said. "He's nothing if not a gentleman."

"Bummer. For a minute I thought he was going to stuff it in Destiny's mouth." Kimmy snickered.

"Good one," said an old man who took a coffee cup out of Kimmy's hand.

We looked at the man as he shuffled away, then at each other, and we both cracked up.

Kimmy wanted to go for a mocha latte after the soup kitchen, but I couldn't wait to get home and start writing. I used the excuse that I had too much homework, which wasn't even a lie.

After the American chop suey incident, Destiny had wanted Spencer to take her home, but evidently Spencer wasn't about to renege on his responsibilities to his team or the people who'd come to be fed. He slipped back into the service line and continued passing out brownies while Destiny huffed, pouted, and sucked on her fingernails on a chair by the entrance, her arms folded over the awful stain. I swear, one time I thought I caught him looking over at Kimmy and me. But Kimmy was all too quick to point out the big round clock above our heads. He had probably just been checking the minutes till quittin' time. But a girl can dream, can't she?

Kimmy's mom dropped me off at Mom's condo. Even though I liked our house better, the condo was like being on vacation. It was newer and more spread out than Dad's house. Everything was on one floor. Sam and I each had our own bathroom, which was a huge plus. No smelly man sprays or jock-itch powder on the floor, drips of pee on the toilet seat, and balled-up towels—aka mold-growing science projects—in the corners. Mom was far neater than Dad, which was more of a problem for Sam than me. There was something soothing about the order of the place, the clean lines of an uncluttered kitchen counter, the way my toes sank into the pile of plush wall-to-wall carpet. Something about the silence, the general lack of creaks and pops, just the hush of warm air being forced through little grates in the wall.

When I got back to the condo, Sam's light was still on.

"Hey, Soph, come in here," he called.

I wasn't in the mood to talk. I just wanted to get to my laptop. I pushed open the door but stayed in the hall. "Hey."

"How was the soup?" he asked.

"What are you talking about?" You know how sometimes just the sight of your brother's face can make you want to punch him?

"You were at a soup kitchen, right?"

I rolled my eyes. "God, there was no *soup!*" I groaned. What a moron. "And even if there was, I wasn't there to eat it. We served pasta to homeless people, okay?" I started to leave.

"What's your problem?" Sam said. "Don't tell me you still hate everyone and everything." He winked.

I mustered a smile. After all, I was being a jerk. "Sorry. I'm just tired and have some homework left to do."

"Better you than me," he said. I noticed Sam's hair was taking on the green tinge that he got from being in chlorinated pools all the time. Fortunately, his swim season was wrapping up.

"G'night," I said. I no sooner made it to my bedroom than Mom appeared at the door.

"How was it?" she asked. She had a glass of white wine in her hand, which usually meant she was in the mood to chat. "Was Spencer there?"

Okay, shoot me for the one time I'd shared too much information. Mom and I had gone for pedicures a couple of weeks earlier. We were hanging out at the mall afterward, and for some reason I'd gotten swept up in the mother-daughter moment and had confessed my secret crush to her. Since then, whenever I came home from anywhere, she asked about Spencer.

"He was there," I said.

"Did you talk to him?"

I rolled my eyes. What happened to make adults so painfully clueless? What post-teenage trauma triggered such a shift in their molecules, their DNA? Did it happen over time or all of a sudden, like one morning they just woke up clueless—*so* clueless they had no idea how clueless they were?

"Okay, forget I asked," Mom said, finally picking up on my annoyance. She shrugged and took a sip of her wine, then smiled and raised her glass to me.

"I'm going to bed," I said. "Love you."

"Love you, too," she echoed.

Alone in my room at last. I fired up my laptop and got into my pajamas and brushed my teeth while it was booting up. What web of deceit would I weave tonight? What adventure?

How many counts does it take to save an African village? Apparently, just one. As promised, informants were on hand to capture the count and his date with destiny. Though what obviously began as an evening with the most sincere and generous intentions turned into a bit of a bloodbath, or at least a catfight. Here's what happened:

S arrived in swanky style with a lovely brunette on his arm, an out-of-towner as far as we could tell. There was plenty of schmoozing over hors d'oeuvres, though no one actually seemed to know who they were.

Count S and his squeeze took their $2,500-a-plate seats toward the front of the dining room. As the ceremony began, donors from around the world were acknowledged: a Dubai businessman, who'd underwritten a wing of the African town's new hospital; a mysterious woman in a blonde wig and oversize sunglasses—who sounded a lot like Cher—who'd donated a veterinary clinic. The list went on until, finally, it was Count S's turn to accept thanks on behalf of his family's charitable foundation for a new school, a new police station, and four years of college tuition to an American university for anyone who graduated high school in the next four years. When the count's name was called, he stood and took a bow, his girlfriend beaming with pride.

That's when all hell broke loose.

Apparently, the count's date had been rude to one of the servers earlier in the evening—an attractive young African woman in tribal dress. As Count S reclaimed his seat, the server, who had been carrying a small tray of drinks, "accidentally" tripped, spilling chocolate martinis all over the count's stunning date. Did we mention she was wearing a white dress?

The sticky girlfriend jumped up and started fanning her lap. Count S dispatched another waiter for some club soda and paper towels. Meanwhile, the girl continued to shriek and sob until the count had to usher her out of the building. An informant reported seeing him slip one of his cards to the lovely African server on his way out. . . . Stay tuned. . . .

P.S. It seems that some of you have never heard of Count S. Allow us to refer, once again, to his overbearing mother and aunts, and an equally overprotective father. Cloistered until his nineteenth birthday, our dear count has only just made it onto the American scene. It will take the paparazzi a while to catch up. They're not as bright as they look. So hang in there, CELEBSTALKER19.

Adoringly, Mlle. Blogger

Before I shut down for the night, I noticed two more comments on the first blog entry. People were actually reading my crazy, made-up story.

The first, from RINGMYBELLE from Charlotte, NC:

Count S sounds dreamy. Does he like Southern girls?

And another from someone closer to home, BOSTONBABE:

So what exactly is a count anyway?

Honestly, heck if I knew. I supposed it was time to do a little research. Tomorrow. Tonight I would drop into bed and dream of my gallant semi-made-up heartthrob.

CHAPTER FOUR

• •

The next day, before school, I noticed a few more comments, including another from CELEBSTALKER19, who had this to say:

> *This count of yours does sound yummy, even to a straight guy like me. I wish you could give us a little more scoop, like where did this charity event take place? It was outside my radar, and I know everything going on from Boston to Beverly Hills.*

I had the feeling CELEBSTALKER19 was going to be a royal pain.

You hear, sometimes, about how stars align for people, things fall into place, and cosmic energy just suddenly shifts. That's what happened. I can't explain it, but as soon as I started blogging about Count S, it was like the fog lifted. Not only did I feel better, but it was as if suddenly people could see me. Of course, no one at school knew what I was doing, not even Kimmy. It was like this bit of information gave me some secret power. I felt a surge of confidence.

So it didn't even bother me a few days later when I got an e-mail from the French consulate that informed me, ever so regrettably, that they would not be able to entertain my request. Somehow, I had moved on from my profound disappointment, at least temporarily.

What do I mean about people suddenly seeing me? Our French teacher was a no-show, so we were told to use the period as a study hall. I had no homework to catch up on and was bored out of my skull, so I opened my notebook and started jotting down ideas for Count S blog entries.

I could feel someone behind me. I didn't think anything of it. Kids were wandering around the classroom. I hunched over my notebook and continued writing. I had some juicy ideas, including a story about Count S being caught making out with a mystery girl at a nightclub I'd heard about and couldn't wait until I was old enough to get into myself.

"Hey."

I knew that voice. I turned around. It was Spencer. He appeared to be talking to me, though I looked over both shoulders anyway, just to be sure.

Even though he was one whole year older than me, Spencer and I were in the same French class. As I mentioned earlier, Spencer is a gifted math student, but his foreign-language skills leave something to be desired, while I, on the other hand, have always excelled in French. That put us in the same class, though I'd only ever worshipped him from across the room. He sat with the rest of the juniors, and he almost never spoke in class unless forced by the teacher.

I wondered how long he'd been looking over my shoulder. My face turned red, and I slammed the notebook shut.

"Hi?" I said. It came out more like a question.

"That was you I saw in front of the house with the Halloween lights the other day. And then you were at the soup kitchen, too, right?" he said. He flipped his hair like I'd seen him do a hundred times, only this time, he was doing it to get the hair out of his eyes so he could see *me*.

"Uh-huh." If only Kimmy were here. She'd never believe it.

"I was trying to figure out where I knew you from. Then I remembered . . . here." He leaned on my desk. I was eye level with his belt buckle and didn't know where to look. He was wearing a white T-shirt under an open plaid button-down shirt with the sleeves rolled up. "That was cool of you and your friend to show up the other night."

I picked at the corner of my notebook. "Well, you know, Kimmy and I, we try to help out," I said, all aw-shucks-y. Of course, my motivation had been slightly less noble. "Besides, we had nothing better to do." *Oh my God, did I really say that?* True as it was, I'd just announced to my crush that I didn't have a life. I felt my face get hot.

"I want to ask you a favor. And you can totally say no." No, I couldn't. Whatever it was—walk through fire, run off to Vegas and get married, give up all my worldly possessions, go stand on my head in the middle of the street, eat chocolate-covered worms—I'd do it.

"What's that?" I braced myself.

"I suck at this. French, I mean." He leaned closer and lowered his voice a little for the next part. My skin went tingly. "If I don't pass this class, I'll have to go to summer school to have enough credits to graduate next spring." He straightened. "So I guess I'm asking if you can help me out. Maybe just once every other week after school or during study. For like an hour or something. I just keep getting more lost."

"Like be your tutor?" *Me? Be Spencer's tutor?*

"Yeah." He smiled. His teeth sparkled.

"Why me?" I asked. I was suspicious. Maybe this was some kind of trick.

"Because you're one of the smartest kids in class. When you speak French, you sound like you grew up there." He seemed sincere. And he did have a point. I was good at French. Though for some reason not good enough to go to Montreal. But I had almost let that go.

"Um, sure, okay." I opened up my agenda and tried to be cool. "When were you thinking?" *Let's see, Spencer Kavanaugh, when can I manage to squeeze you in?*

"I have a math team meet this week—they're every other Wednesday, now till the end of school—and then lacrosse the other days, but I was thinking maybe next Wednesday? After school? I could meet you in the library."

I looked down at my calendar, at the little square for next Wednesday. It was blissfully empty. "That works."

"That's awesome, thanks." He hesitated and suddenly seemed embarrassed. "I can't really afford to pay you but . . ."

"Like I said, I like to help out when I can." *Pay me?* I should be the one doing the paying.

Spencer went back to his seat. My pen was shaking in my hand. It was all too inconceivable. He recognized me in front of my house and then at the soup kitchen, and therefore knew I existed. And not only did he know who I was, but he knew I was *good* at something.

And now, incredibly, I would be his French tutor!

The feeling that my head had been replaced by a helium balloon didn't go away until last period, when it struck me: how would I ever keep it together for an hour in such close proximity to Spencer? Suddenly, writing about my imaginary Count S seemed much safer than an actual encounter with an actual heartthrob.

Later that day I saw Sam in the hall, leaning on the lockers, actually talking to Michelle Alberghetti, and she, in turn, seemed genuinely interested. A fine day of firsts for the Delorme twins, it seemed.

I knew I had to think about something for the next week other than my upcoming tutoring session with Spencer or I would go insane. I could have asked Dad what he knew about French nobility but, honestly, I didn't want to dredge up the whole unpleasant business again. So I hit the Internet to find out more about what a count was.

I learned that the word comes from the French *comte*, which is derived from the Latin *comes*, which originally meant "companion" and later "companion of the *emperor*." Interestingly enough, the position was not originally hereditary. By holding large estates during the Middle Ages, many counts were able to hang on to their titles. In prerevolutionary France, the noble class enjoyed monetary and other privileges, some of which Dad had mentioned, like the rights to hunt and wear swords, the holding of coats of arms, and exemptions from paying certain taxes. In exchange, nobles were required to honor, serve, and counsel their king. These days, the title of count is purely honorary and confers no legal privileges.

Much of what I read was quick to point out that nobility should not be confused with socioeconomic status. Our family was living proof of that.

I also learned that the *de* before a French last name often signifies nobility, though it isn't something that's been officially controlled in France, the way *von* has been in Germany. After privileges were done away with during the French Revolution, Napoleon tried to resurrect the old titles, which, according to French historians, sort of cheapened the whole thing.

At least I had enough now hopefully to appease BOSTONBABE. And my own curiosity.

> Stop the presses. (Does anyone even know what *presses* are?) The wild rumor circulating is that Count S has taken up with his English translator, a proper French girl who wears Chanel and grew up outside of Paris. Sources say she moved to Manhattan just months ago and, being from Europe, is well acquainted with Count S and his European preeminence.
>
> According to a New York informant, S was seen on the streets of Greenwich Village using his translator to converse with a group of hot pajama-clad NYU coeds. They were in the middle of a conversation about nightclubs, the translator relaying their recommendations to him, when, ignoring the other girls, Count S reached over and cradled her face in both hands, then kissed her on the lips with a passion that would make Jennifer

Aniston's hair curl. The informant, who happened on the
scene as he exited a coffee shop, stood and watched
them carry on until his tea went tepid. The two then
disappeared into an apartment building, and the
informant went home to take a cold shower.

One last relevant bit of information: according to his
teachers at the lycée back home, Count S speaks
perfect English.

Adoringly, Mlle. Blogger

Sunday afternoon Mom dropped us back at the house. I noticed that
Dad's car wasn't in the driveway.

Obviously, Sam did not. He ran up the stairs, burst through the
front door, and hollered, "Dad!"

Sam liked going back to the house even more than I did. For
starters, he could dump his stuff in a heap at the bottom of the
stairs, whereas Mom always made us bring our things directly to
our rooms and unpack and organize for the entire week before we
could even get something to eat. Here, life was just a little freer all
around.

I followed Sam into the kitchen. "Dad, we're home!" he yelled.

Something was different. I couldn't quite put my finger on it.
"He's not here," I said. "His car wasn't in the driveway."

"Oh." Sam already had the refrigerator door open, his head
inside. He grabbed a cheese stick and an apple. "Nothing even
remotely edible in here." He slammed the door shut.

Dad hadn't stocked up on groceries yet. That was probably where he was. So what was different? Taylor's coffee grinder wasn't on the counter. And her windowsill Chia herb garden, which never got moved, even when Mom came around, was gone.

"Where's Taylor's stuff?" I said.

"Huh?" Sam had already polished off the string cheese and had just taken an enormous bite of the apple.

"Wake up! Did you smell her hair stuff when we came in? I didn't."

"Have I ever smelled her hair stuff? That's such a chick question," Sam said. "Maybe she didn't stay here this week. Big deal." He sat down at the kitchen table and put his feet on a chair. "Maybe Mom was here earlier. You know the drill."

I was surprised that *he* knew the drill. "Taylor never takes the plants. Dad just pretends they're his." I riffled through Dad's stack of junk mail, as if I were expecting something addressed to me. I tossed the pile back on the counter, threw Sam's stinky feet off the chair, and sat down. "So what's up with you and Michelle, Queen of Putnam?" I asked, probing.

Sam had been about to take another chunk out of the apple. He stopped mid-bite, his lips still curled around the skin. "What? Nothing."

"Don't *nothing* me. I saw you talking by the lockers last week. And she was actually looking *interested*." I leaned forward and mustered my most sinister smile. "So what's with that?"

He set the demolished apple down on a grocery store circular and wiped his mouth with his sleeve. Why was he looking so sheepish? Suddenly, it dawned on me.

I stood up. "You didn't tell her about the family stuff!"

Sam looked down. "No!" he shouted, maybe protesting a little too much. I knew my brother better than anyone.

"Sam, you promised!"

"I didn't tell her about the count thing. *Honest*."

"Then what *did* you tell her?" I demanded. With my hands on my hips, I towered over him.

Sam looked down at the ravaged fruit. "I might have mentioned something about some euros in a French bank," he admitted. He looked up and winced a little, then added, "And maybe something about a château."

"Oh my *God*." I stomped away from the table. "You are such an idiot."

"What difference does it make?"

I thought about the blog and the virtual impossibility of anyone at Putnam High ever reading it. Even if someone did, they'd never make any connection. I had been careful to hide my identity. I supposed that beyond the fact that I was jealous that Sam got the title and I didn't, whether he talked about it at school didn't really matter at all. Plus, he hadn't even said anything incriminating. Still, I wasn't about to let him off the hook.

"You're a fool, Sam," I said. Only now it was the protective-sister thing kicking in. "You want a girl who will only give you the time of day because she thinks you have some European connection? Or that you might secretly be wealthy?"

"I just want a girl," he said. "*That* girl."

I looked at my brother. He looked so forlorn. His cheeks were red, his eyes cast down so that all I could see were his long eyelashes.

"There are tons of girls at school who think you're a catch."
Saying that made me throw up in my mouth a little. "I mean it," I
added. It was certainly true enough.

"I can't help who I like, Soph," he finally said.

I supposed I couldn't argue with that. "Just do me a favor and
don't tell her anything more."

"I won't. I promise."

I started for my room. "And bring your junk upstairs, okay?"
God, I had become my mother.

Sorry it's been a couple of days. Our dear S isn't the easiest
fellow to keep up with. Just ask his old girlfriend, the
English translator. But trust us, this tidbit is worth the wait.

Rumor has it Count S has holed up with a Saudi princess
in a room at a Boston hotel we're not at "liberty" to
mention. The girl's father is threatening to launch an oil
embargo against France if she doesn't return home by the
end of the week, though that comes from a most unreliable
source. However, our informant at the hotel said she's a
beauty, with long black hair and eyes the color of Arabian
desert sand, and lucky for the count, she's eighteen.
According to someone on the staff, the couple pitched a
tent made of sheets in the suite and have been ordering
up exotic Middle Eastern delicacies, including camel
kabobs, figs, kefta, and hummus. What, no dates? Who
needs dates when you have a Saudi princess in
your room? And something called bride's fingers, a

phyllo-almond confection, which probably tastes a lot better than it sounds. But leave it to Count S to express the need for more than ten lovely fingers on his person at any one time.

With the week's-end deadline looming, we imagine the two lovebirds will have to leave the nest soon. Or France will be running on fumes.

Adoringly, Mlle. Blogger

When I wrote that, I was, of course, imagining what it would be like to be an Arabian princess holed up in a hotel room with Spencer, eating bride's fingers (which Saad Abbas's mother had brought to history class in fourth grade). I'd never have the courage to write about those sorts of things in real life. But through Count S, I was free to write anything. Just as my count was free to do anything, because he was, after all, a count, if an imaginary one.

As for the comments to the blog, they were still accumulating. People were posting from all over the world. They wanted to know how tall he was (five eleven), what kind of car he drove (a Lamborghini . . . had to do a Web search for the spelling), how many siblings he had (none), what his favorite food was (chateaubriand, sea urchin, American pizza), what kind of music he listened to (ska, death metal, Radiohead), what color his eyes were (smoked almond). One girl from Milwaukee wanted to know what celebrity he most resembled. (Spencer Kavanaugh . . . What, never heard of him? Okay, so I just ignored that question.) Another wanted to know if he had a dog. (No dog. An Ashera, which is an exotic breed of cat that looks like a leopard and runs around twenty-five grand. [Searched "most expensive cat."] Of course, he also had a run-of-the-mill tiger cat like Calvo, a calico, and a slew of barn kitties at the château to even out his pet karma.) What religion was he? (Nonpracticing Catholic.) What was his shoe size? (Ten and a half.) What did he do for exercise? (Polo, distance running, weight training, and yoga. No lacrosse. That would have been too obvious.)

I realized it was taking me longer to answer these questions than it did to write the entries themselves. But I sort of appreciated having to answer them, because they forced me to flesh out my count in my own mind and make him even more real. Still, I wondered how I was getting so many hits in such a short time. I searched "Count S" online and, sure enough, mine was the first site to come up. Right beneath it was a site with the title celebstalker.com. I clicked on the link, and it seemed my New York friend had jumped on the Count S bandwagon, devoting a small space in the upper left corner of his home page to a few paraphrased lines from my site, all under the title *Mystery Count Capers*. From what I could tell, his was a site that focused less on the Hollywood scene and more on Eurotrash and outing the rich and famous nightclubbing foreigners so that commoners like us could know who we were grinding up against on the dance floor—at least, those of us who were old enough to get into the clubs. CELEBSTALKER19 was careful about quoting my entries, attributing them to an anonymous source and once or twice challenging their veracity, presumably to cover his own butt. Still, I was flattered. Celebstalker.com was a big-time celebrity gossip site with corporate sponsors, and it had taken me virtually no time to break in to it. Count S was becoming more real each day. To me and, seemingly, to the rest of the world.

Dad finally came home with the groceries. When I heard him, I went downstairs.

"There you are," I said. I walked over and gave him a peck on the cheek. He had more whiskers on his face than usual and they scratched my lips.

"Hey, hon," he said. "How was your week?" He started unpacking. Turkey chili, soup, olives, pasta, frozen chicken, dried lentils, bags of whole wheat tortilla chips, and the famous always-on-sale cookies.

"Not bad." I started putting things away. "Actually, pretty darn good."

He kept on unpacking. "How's that?"

First the blog, then my new tutoring pupil. As if I could tell him about either. "I don't know. Some weeks are just better than others," I said. "You know how it is."

"That's the truth," he said. He shook his head. His plaid shirt was wrinkled and untucked in the back, and he looked a little disheveled in general, which made me wonder if my hunch about Taylor was right. Something was up. "How's your mother?" he asked.

"Fine. Same as always. Working her butt off."

"Hmmm," he said. He seemed distracted.

"Mind if I open the cookies?" I asked.

"Be my guest."

I took a cookie and ate it over the sink. "Where's Taylor's Chia garden?"

Dad turned around. I saw for the first time that his eyes were red, like he hadn't slept. "She took it back to her place," he said.

"How come?" I asked.

Dad folded the first paper bag and launched into unpacking the next. Whole wheat bread, canned tuna, eggs, dried cat food, shredded mozzarella . . .

He didn't answer, so I continued. "The same reason the coffee grinder is gone? Did Mom come around or something?"

Dad stopped. He looked stricken. "Was I really that bad?"

I felt a pang in my stomach that sort of flared out to my chest. "What do you mean?" I asked. But I knew what he meant. And at that moment I knew he and Taylor had had a fight and Taylor had bounced.

He turned back around. "Never mind."

I couldn't let it go. "Yes, you were that bad. Every time Mom comes over, it's like you want to erase Taylor from the house. It doesn't make sense. Mom knows about Taylor. You guys have been apart for four years. You don't have to pretend you don't have a girlfriend. Taylor acts like it doesn't bother her most of the time, but it has to," I said. "So is that it? She's gone? And that's why?"

Dad dropped his chin to his chest. "Sometimes it doesn't feel like four years. Sometimes it feels like yesterday."

I walked over and gave my poor wounded father a hug. "Maybe Taylor will come around," I said. But I knew it was Dad who needed to come around—to accepting that his marriage was over. He needed to move on, once and for all. I couldn't blame Taylor for leaving. "Let me make dinner tonight," I said as I pulled away from him.

"That's okay." There were tears in his eyes.

"No really, I want to."

Dad had gone upstairs after what had been a painfully silent dinner. I had filled Sam in beforehand so he wouldn't say anything to make things worse. Now I was washing and Sam was drying, seeing as our dishwasher hadn't worked in three years.

"So you think now Mom and Dad will get back together?" Sam asked.

Was he for real? I dropped the sponge in the sink and looked at him. *"Really?"*

"Okay, I know. That was stupid."

I felt no need to rub it in. After all, the thought had crossed my own mind for a fleeting instant. I grabbed a scrubby sponge and started on the goo at the bottom of a saucepan. "Taylor was good for Dad," I said.

"She was chill." (That's a good thing, FYI.)

"And she loves him."

Sam set the plate he was drying on the countertop and picked up another from the drainboard. "So what do you think happened?"

"My guess is that she got tired of playing the other woman." I turned on the water and let it rinse the soap from my pan.

"Huh?"

"I just mean the way Dad tried to keep his whole relationship on the down low, trying to sneak around so his ex-wife wouldn't know. I mean, how would that make anyone feel?" I said.

"Not great." Sam grabbed a handful of silverware.

"But I think Dad really does love her. I just think he's never fully let go of Mom."

"Maybe you should talk to her."

I rested my wrists on the edge of the sink and looked at Sam. "Who, Mom?"

"Taylor. You guys always had a bond. That chick thing."

"Would you please stop calling me a chick?" I said.

"Would you please stop calling me an *idiot*?"

That was simply too much to ask. "Okay, never mind. Call me a chick." I started on the colander.

"Nice," Sam said. He tried to snap my backside with the towel and missed.

"If it's any consolation, talking to her may not be such an idiotic idea. Dad is miserable, so it would at least help to know if we're even in the ballpark on all this."

"Kimmy, you'll never believe what happened." I was on my bed, talking on the phone, my head resting on my big red fuzzy-lips pillow. "Taylor left Dad. We got here this afternoon and all her stuff was gone."

"Get *out*," Kimmy said. "That's awful. You like her, right?"

"I guess." I'd only just realized how much recently. I thought about our conversation on the steps and how she'd tried to make me feel better. I wondered if she was writing about her breakup with Dad now.

Speaking of writing, I heard keyboard clacking through the phone.

"Are you Facebooking while you're talking to me?" I asked.

"No. Sorry." The clacking stopped. "I mean, I *was*, but I'm not now."

I thought I was bad, but Kimmy was a total computer addict,

always searching for the latest viral sensations, sharing site addresses and posts. Recently I had been too busy with my own blog even to keep up with her Facebook page, which had a pretty decent following at school, even with the popular kids. Though for some reason, her coolness didn't translate beyond cyberspace. Kids never gave her the credit for finding things. They just reposted her posts. But Kimmy didn't seem to care. All she cared about was how many people were viewing her pages. In a way, she'd created as much of an online persona as I had with my Count S blog. It sort of killed me that I couldn't tell her what I was doing, but I was just too afraid to tell anyone.

"Do you know what you're going to do with Spencer on Wednesday?" Kimmy asked. "Besides lust after him."

"I've been gathering up some lesson ideas," I said. Actually, I had already spent most of the weekend trying to figure it out. Thank goodness we were on an every-other-week schedule or I'd flunk out of my own classes.

"Someone posted a link to this incredible picture of a pregnant belly with a tiny foot imprint pressing through from the inside." Kimmy was obviously still online.

"Kimmy, please. I just ate."

"And I found a new blog. It tracks Jessica Simpson's weight fluctuations."

"That's mean." My eyes wandered to my dresser and landed on a photo of me, Dad, and Taylor at a restaurant. "But sort of interesting." Dad looked happy.

"Do you think there's any hope of your dad and Taylor getting back together?" It was as if Kimmy had read my mind.

"I don't know. Sam says I should talk to Taylor. I have no idea what I'd say, mostly because I can't blame her for leaving."

"Maybe it's your father who needs a talking-to."

"Yeah," I said. Since when was it up to an almost sixteen-year-old to try to fix her dad's broken heart?

CHAPTER FIVE

• •

At some point I realized I hadn't taken a breath for close to ten minutes. As soon as we'd sat down, I had opened the French notebook and just started rattling off the lesson I had painstakingly prepared. My voice sounded like something piped through a pastry tube, thin and sugary. All week long I had imagined this moment, and now here I was, having this out-of-body experience where I was floating up by the ceiling, looking down at Spencer and me sitting together on the same side of the table, our knees almost touching. The whole side of my body closest to him felt feverish. I kept stumbling over my words (though he was too horrible at French even to notice). Finally, the lack of oxygen caught up with me. I gasped.

"You okay?" he asked.

I feigned a cough and sucked in some air. "Dry throat." I popped another Altoid, perhaps the twentieth of the day in preparation for Spencer's first tutoring session in the library. Could a person overdose on Altoids?

"Want one?" I asked. I held out the box.

He shook his head. "No, thanks. Hate those."

Great. I'd been spewing peppermint breath at him all this time and he hated Altoids. I swallowed the mint whole.

"Okay, so let's use that," I said. I had started with the workbook from class but soon realized we needed to go back a year to review some of the basics. I had been reading from a chapter on food. "So I say, *'Qu'est-ce que tu aimes manger?'* Then what do you say?"

His hair was still damp. He must've just taken a shower after gym class. He smelled like soap, the manly kind. "Je . . . em . . ."

Say it! Just say it, Spencer. Je t'aime, *Sophie. I love you. It's always been you!* Steady, girl. "You say, *'Je n'aime pas manger les* Altoids.' Try it."

"Je . . . name . . . paw . . . manger . . . less . . . Altoids." (Even the *Altoids* had been butchered.)

"Oui, très bien!" I said.

After about a half hour, I settled down, realizing that Spencer was, in fact, not a demigod but a human being, and a flawed one at that. His French was horrible, perhaps even borderline hopeless. It was up to me to single-handedly rescue his future. I took the responsibility to heart.

It was probably my imagination, but a couple of times I thought I caught him looking up at me. But he was probably just bored and looking around. Still, I had a hunch there was something else on his mind.

We were getting near the end of the lesson when he put his pen in the crease of the workbook and pushed it away. "Can I ask you something?" He didn't wait for me to say yes. "If you were a girl—"

If I were a girl? Really? My face must've betrayed me.

He backpedaled. "I *know* you're a girl. I mean, from a girl's perspective, what's a cool thing for a guy to write in a girl's yearbook?" Yearbooks had been passed out in homerooms that morning. Now we would begin the arduous task of trying to get people to sign them. Arduous, at least for those of us who were less than popular. I had contemplated asking Spencer to sign my book that afternoon, which was why it now sat on the table. But I hadn't yet mustered the nerve. Maybe in another two weeks I would.

I was a little confused by his question. "You want to know how to write something in French?" I asked.

"English." He pushed away from the table and turned his chair to face me. "Take off your tutor hat now. Just be a girl."

"I'll try." I glared at him. "Is this someone you like or just a friend?" Every fiber in my body was hoping for door number two.

"A friend, I guess. But I sort of like her. I mean, I could see it turning into more someday."

Fantastic. Did he really need my help with this? If there was one person in this school who knew what to say to a girl . . . and yet he seemed serious.

I closed my workbook. "I don't know, just be flirty. Leave it kind of open-ended, you know?"

"Like . . ."

"*Like* say something nice about her eyes or her hair or something, and then—"

He looked more lost than my father had that time I needed underwear and dragged him into Victoria's Secret. "Seriously, you want me to write it *for* you?" I was annoyed, and with good reason. Of course, Spencer couldn't know I wanted to bear his children. "How about this: 'Dear so and so, I just want to tell you . . . I think you have the perfect . . . ,' then fill in the blank . . . smile, dimples, lips, though nothing too anatomically intimate, if you get my drift." I felt my cheeks heat up. "Then maybe something like 'I need to know you better.'"

Spencer smiled. "That's pretty awesome."

"Thanks. Do you mind if we get back to the French? I have to be somewhere soon," I lied.

"Continue-ay," he said. He winked, and all was forgiven, even the part about me being a girl.

Moments later, we were packing up our books. I was proud of myself. I'd been a good teacher and I thought I'd really helped him. It made me feel good.

"Really appreciate this, Sophie," he said. "You obviously worked a lot to prepare."

Ah, my name, how lovely it sounded rolling off his tongue. I sighed, then cleared my throat to cover. "No problem," I said. "Same time two weeks from today?" I stuffed my French workbooks and my yearbook into my backpack.

"Absolut-i-ment."

God, he was so bad it was adorable.

News flash. The parents of Count S have split. This update from an expat informant across the pond, who picked up the item in a French tabloid. After thirty years, the mother has run off with a German banker, and the marquis is inconsolable. We'll have to wait and see how the fallout affects Count S, and whether he'll go back to France to be with his dad, travel to Germany to try to wrest his mother from the banker, or stay here and lick his wounds with the help of any of a number of women who'd rally for the chance.

The count was last seen in a nightclub parking lot, locking lips with a beautiful blonde woman—an NFL cheerleader—in what is becoming a rather routine public display of affection. Is this acting out a sign of things to come?

Adoringly, Mlle. Blogger

They say truth is stranger than fiction. Actually, there was nothing strange about what I saw in the school parking lot. The high school "royals" can quite often be seen hanging out by their cars. Still, that didn't prepare me for the sight of Spencer with not Destiny, but that blonde cheerleader who'd also been in the car with him that day he drove past my house. This must be the yearbook girl. Kimmy and I were making another Skittles run when we happened upon the scene. It was starting to drizzle.

"Don't ask questions. Just look ahead and keep walking," Kimmy said.

Naturally, I stopped and looked around. There they were, just ahead. As we got closer, I saw Spencer pinned against the truck.

"Jeez," I said. I wished we'd taken the sidewalk rather than cutting through the parking lot.

"I said don't look!" Kimmy tugged on my sleeve.

"That's that cheerleader," I said. "I saw her in his car the week before last."

"I'm wondering if we should call 911. He looks like he's being attacked." That was Kimmy, always trying to make me feel better.

"What is it, Kimmy? How come guys like that always go for girls like *that*?" I wiped the rain from my face. "How come they never go for girls like me?"

"Don't look now, but he's spotted us. Oh my God. And he's pushing the girl away," Kimmy said.

This time I kept my head down. I wanted to believe it, but I didn't dare look. My face was on fire.

"Don't toy with me, Kimmy."

"I'm not. He totally did."

A girl in lust goes to great lengths to protect her infatuation. So while I was devastated but not surprised to see Spencer with that girl, I allowed myself to focus on the ever-so-remote possibility that he actually *had* pushed yearbook cheerleader away when he'd seen Kimmy and me. And I left it at that. I wasn't going to imagine that he was ashamed or embarrassed or secretly pining for me but making do with the hottest cheerleader in school because I was, what . . . unavailable? Right. See, if I went too far down that road, my illusion fell apart.

And on the topic of illusions falling apart, I was in a rotten mood, having spent the last hour reading all the flirty entries in Spencer's yearbook. I realized yesterday after our tutoring session that we'd accidently switched books. I had brought his to school today to give back, but he'd been pulled out of class for a lacrosse away game. And tomorrow we had an assembly, so no French class.

I didn't think he'd bother to look through mine, but even if he did, the only kids I'd gotten to sign it so far were Kimmy and

Jimmy Tucker, the guy who'd let us get his car cleaned, and neither had written anything incriminating. Spencer's book, on the other hand, had already been autographed by the most popular girls in the junior class, and even some seniors, all having penned precisely the kinds of suggestive things I'd told him to write in the mystery girl's yearbook. It was depressing.

But I had to put my heartache aside for now. I had more important things to think about, like the sanity of my father. I had asked Taylor to meet me at the house. She'd agreed, as long as Dad wasn't home. She said she had stuff to pick up, anyway.

The sky was still spitting, so I waited for Taylor on the porch swing, realizing too late that I'd sat on Sam's Easter candy stash and flattened his marshmallow Peeps. I moved to the other side, closed my eyes, and let the subtle motion of the swing lull me to sleep. I was just about out when I heard Taylor coming up the stairs.

"Hey," she said. "You awake?"

I blinked my eyes open. "Hey." I sat up. "Just resting."

Taylor looked like she'd just come from a yoga class. She had on black stretch pants, her goofy red blunt-toe leather Mary Janes with the rubber soles, and a hippieish white hoodie made of gauze, which came down almost to her knees. She was wearing a black headband, and her crazy brown hair was pulled back in an elastic, half in, half out. She came over and gave me a kiss on the forehead.

"Where's your father?" she asked.

"He had to go into the office today."

I could see her shoulders relax. She started to sit down next to me.

"Wait! I don't think you want to do that," I cautioned.

"Huh?" she stood.

"Sam's candy stash," I explained. "I just killed some chicks. Lord knows what else he's got under there. Wanna go inside?"

"Okay," she said. She waited until I'd gotten up, then followed me in. I led her over to the kitchen counter. For the first time, I was actually a little embarrassed for Dad. The place was a mess. On the window ledge were books and newspapers and a plate with a half-eaten bagel. On the table were a knife with peanut butter on it, spilled salt, and a few of my hair elastics, which I snatched up and stuffed into my pocket.

It wasn't as if Taylor wasn't used to the house being a mess. She'd practically lived here herself. But for the first time, I was seeing it through someone else's eyes. If Dad ever wanted to land a woman, he needed to clean up his act.

"Have a seat," I said.

"Thank you," Taylor replied. She was smiling, but she still looked sad.

I brushed the salt into my hand and dumped it on the floor. "Look. I know my dad isn't the easiest guy to live with," I started. "In fact, he can be downright dense about things, but—"

"Sophie. I love your father," Taylor said.

I realized I was still looking at the salt on the floor. I looked up into her eerie blue eyes, and they were pooled with tears. "But then how come—"

"It's him," she said. "He can't let go."

"Of what?" Though I knew where this was headed.

"Your mother. His family. The past. All of it."

"But he does love you. I'm sure of it."

She pushed back from the table. "You know what? I think he does. But he's paralyzed. And wounded. And I can't keep waiting for him to come around. Because what if he doesn't?"

I got up and threw my arms around her. I think she was a little surprised at first, but then she settled into the hug, and we both sort of cried on each other's shoulders.

Finally, I pulled away. I ran my sleeve across my face. "Don't totally give up, Taylor. I'll talk to him."

"I appreciate that, Sophie, but I've talked to him a hundred times and it hasn't helped. He's just stuck. And I don't think anything can unstick him."

After Taylor left, I went into my room and closed the door. I didn't feel like talking to anyone, least of all Dad. Fortunately, he called to say he was meeting a friend at a campus pub after work and wouldn't be home until after dinner. I checked my e-mail, and there was a message from Kimmy about some earth-shattering new blog to check out. I'd do it later, if I remembered.

I went to my own site, just to take my mind off things. There were at least twenty new comments, from all over. Rather than reproduce the list, I'll give you the highlights.

From FRANCAISKAY, in Hoboken, NJ:

> *My parents split, too. If the count needs a shoulder to cry on, let me know.*

Another from RINGMYBELLE, in Charlotte, NC:

Count S's mother sounds like a nightmare.

And from my new worst best friend:

I'm afraid I have some bad news. I assume the hint on a former post was that Count S had been staying at the Liberty Hotel in Boston. I checked with the management there. Your story couldn't be confirmed. I'm sure it's just some misunderstanding. But we're all wondering.

CELEBSTALKER19 was turning into Sophie stalker!

And one more. From MARRYRICH in Santa Monica, CA:

Is the marquis good-looking, too? I like older men.

Sam knocked on my door. I clicked the browser window closed as he came in without bothering to wait for a reply.

"I saw Taylor leave. What did she say?" He was dressed like he'd come straight from gym class.

"What's *that?*" I pointed to what looked like a black dinner plate under my brother's armpit.

"Never seen a Frisbee before?" He pretended to fling it at my head. "Come outside and help me practice."

"Practice? What in the world are you doing with a Frisbee?" I asked. "What about swim team?"

"Swimming's almost over. I'm going out for coed ultimate. Come on."

I got up, reluctantly, and followed him down the stairs. Frisbee or not, the fresh air would do me good. *"Really?"* I said. "I wonder who else is on that team." I already knew Michelle Alberghetti was.

"Shut up." And apparently, he knew I knew. "So tell me what Taylor said."

"Taylor thinks Dad is hopeless. I'm starting to agree."

Sam pushed open the screen door. I followed him down the stairs to the front lawn. "What's that supposed to mean?" He pointed to where I should stand.

I followed his finger. "It means Dad's stuck in the past. He's afraid to move on with his life. And he's willing to toss out a great relationship with a really cool person because he's too thick in the head to realize it."

"Speaking of toss . . . catch!" Sam let the Frisbee go with a sharp flick of his wrist. It spun through the air. I watched in helpless awe as it hit me on the shoulder, shot off, and scraped along the sidewalk until it finally came to a stop in the gutter. "Nice one," he said.

"Give me a break." I retrieved the Frisbee and hit it against my hip like a tambourine to get off the dust and gravel.

"So it's him. It's not her. I mean, if he came around, she'd probably come back?" Sam asked. Then, in a sharper tone, "Throw it already, will you?"

"Maybe, but she's been pretty patient until now." I altered my stance, this time moving my right foot a little forward. I held the Frisbee by the rim, drew back my arm, and let it fly, hopping forward on one foot as it shot off toward the porch, smashed one of the Halloween lights on the column, then wobbled toward Sam. He caught it.

"Sheesh, Sophie." He shook his head and launched.

I braced myself for another hit. This time, the Frisbee soared over my head, then drifted back. How did he get to be so good at this? He was always better at sports than I was. He picked things up on the first try. Like that time Dad took us to hit golf balls and Sam did great, while I wound up with a welt on my ankle that, to this day, I can't explain. Now, I'd be damned if I didn't catch this pass. That's what was going through my head as, almost in slow motion, the Frisbee hit the knuckles of my right hand and fell to the grass.

"Ouch!" I picked up the evil black disk.

"Just relax, will you?" Sam took a baseball catcher's stance. "Right here," he said. He patted his chest. "I don't think we should give up. I think you should talk to Dad."

"Me?" I gripped the Frisbee, drew back my arm, and let loose. "Why *me*?" This time, I let go too soon and hooked it to the left, over the street and into the closed window of the neighbor's parked car, from which it bounced into their hedges. Calvo hissed and scurried out from the base of the bushes. Apparently, I had interrupted his catnap.

"Okay. We're done," Sam said. He ran across the street, stuck his hand in the bushes, and retrieved his Frisbee, then brushed off the dirt. "Look, you're the one who talked to Taylor."

"Only because you said I should."

"Besides, I can't talk to Dad about stuff like that. You're a girl. You can give him some perspective." At least with Sam I didn't have to imagine being a girl.

"One more time, come on," I said. I raised my hand. Sam was still in the street. He looked both ways. No cars were coming. He shot the Frisbee straight up into the air so that it came down vertically at a really fast clip, right toward my head. I put my hands over my scalp and ducked. The Frisbee missed by no more than a few inches.

"Are you trying to kill me?!"

Sam shook his head. "It's a Frisbee, Soph. You're supposed to *catch* it. Or at least try." He tucked the disk back under his arm and headed for his Easter stash.

Those last words of Sam's stuck with me as I went back upstairs to my desk. I had a choice. I could squeeze my eyes shut, press my hands over my ears, and duck. Metaphorically speaking, that is. I could accept that Dad was a grown man and there was nothing I could do.

Or I could at least try to help. I had no idea what to say, but I owed Dad and Taylor that much. And as much as I felt Sam was sleazing his way out of this one, I knew he was right. This was a conversation that needed to be had between father and daughter.

> Dearest Celebstalker19, Do you really think the count and his Arabian princess would have used their real names to check in to a hotel?
>
> Adoringly, Mlle. Blogger

Almost immediately, I received this message:

No bride's fingers on the room service menu.

So I replied:

LYNN KIELE BONASIA

Ever hear of takeout?

Which he seemed to ignore:

That week the entire hotel had been rented out for a software convention.

Hmmm. Panic. Now what? Why, all of a sudden, had it become so important that I keep up this charade? Forget the followers I'd amassed. The very life of my fictional character was at stake, a character who was some kind of amalgam of what I wanted and what I wasn't. I was invested. I had to see what S would do next. Because in some bizarre way, it was as if I had something to learn from him. It was as simple as that.

Saturday he posted:

Sweetie, your credibility is on the line. Throw me a bone. Give me something that shows this count even exists. I'm losing faith.
—CELEBSTALKER19

In the wee hours of Monday morning, I posted:

Is this the kind of proof you were looking for?

CHAPTER SIX

. . . .

Sam's room at Mom's wasn't much different from Sam's room at Dad's, except that everything was newer and more color coordinated, and there wasn't as much junk on the floor, because Mom made him clean up at the end of each stay. So now, as I tiptoed through the doorway, I was less worried about what I might trip over or what diseases I might catch. But this wasn't like the time I'd wandered into his room with the butter knife; this was a more sinister mission.

I knew precisely where it was—the same place where it had sat since we arrived at Mom's—on the bedside table. The box was open and propped up on a book so the family signet ring faced the bed, as if Sam wanted it to be the last thing he saw each night before he shut his eyes. I'm not even sure how he ever persuaded Dad to let him borrow it. So much for Sam's nonchalance about his title. He probably kissed the ring every morning, too.

And speaking of my brother's weird and pathetic attachments, Sam now slept with his arm thrown over that black Frisbee that had conked me on the head. As I stood over him, his reddish-gold lashes fluttered. I felt a twinge in my gut that spiderwebbed out to my hands. He sensed I was there. The Esses, and that twin thing again.

Focus. Let's get on with this.

I reached in with two fingers and dislodged the ring from its worn red-velvet groove. I clutched it in my palm and slipped out into the hall.

"Sophie, are you still up?" I jumped. It was Mom calling from her room in her "sleepy mom" voice. How did she always know it was me and not Sam? Because Sam slept like the dead, while I had well-documented insomniac tendencies. Fair enough.

"Just going to the bathroom," I called. I matched her sleepy voice and raised her a yawn.

"Hmmm," she replied. I knew she'd be back in the arms of George Clooney in a matter of seconds.

The photo studio was already set up and ready to go. It consisted of a desk lamp with a hundred-watt bulb aimed at a piece of eleven-by-seventeen-inch white copier paper curved in front of the printer and held in place with Scotch tape—the same setup I'd used to shoot my collection of fast-food promotional toys, which I'd finally unloaded on eBay a year earlier. (Do you have any idea how much a complete set of Disney *Tarzan* figures still in their bags will fetch these days?)

I set the ring down on the paper and adjusted the light. I had to admit, it was pretty cool to think how old the thing was and, for something so old, how kind of modern the design was. I felt a pang of jealousy that Sam should be the one to get it, and not just it, but everything that went along with it. *Let it go, girl.*

I grabbed my camera, stepped back, and snapped a few shots of the ring from different angles. I took the three best and uploaded them to my computer. Only I didn't like how they looked. Too stark, like something on Craigslist. I slipped the ring onto my own skinny finger, but it hung loose and, besides, having it on a girl's finger didn't make sense. I needed to come up with a better idea. I sat down on the end of the bed I'd earlier caught an earful from Mom for not making. *Wait a minute!* I set the ring down in the rumpled white sheets. *Perfect!*

I snapped a few close-ups and chose the sexiest one with the clearest view of the crest peeking out above the folds. I uploaded it onto my blog, at the end of my most recent post, along with a few sentences about how the ring had been found in the sheets by a chambermaid, then placed on the bedside table for safekeeping, though not before it had been properly documented. My imaginary informants were apparently not just incredibly thorough, but honest, too.

There it was: photographic proof of Count S's lineage. Now CELEBSTALKER19 would have to back off.

And he did. For the next five days, I heard nothing from my nemesis. Blissful silence. Not to say that there was no feedback from my new bevy of e-friends. Quite the contrary. The crest seemed to have reinvigorated their interest. With CELEBSTALKER19 out of the picture, and feeling unencumbered, I began to spin my heart out.

> The count has left the building or, in this case, the country.
> Just temporarily, we hope. He's crossed the pond to be
> with his father since his parents' split. Turns out there's
> more to that story, too. See, the marquis is now reported
> to have screwed up royally. Those close to him would

attest to the fact that he's always been a bit of a cold fish. Now we're hearing he never gave the dear marquise what she needed, which was merely a dose of love and appreciation. Is that too much to ask? And so she sought it elsewhere. Who can blame her? French women are a passionate lot. And speaking of passionate, the count is reported to have hooked up with a former classmate from the lycée, the daughter of a resort owner on Saint Bart's.

Adoringly, Mlle. Blogger

Where did I come up with this stuff? The Saint Bart's part at least. The rest was rather obvious.

From BITTERSUE from Nantucket, MA:

Men are so clueless.

From DOROTHY32 in Encino, CA:

I've always wanted to go to St. Bart's. I hear there's a nude beach on the south side of the island.

From QUEENBEE on Fire Island, NY (who I suspected was a dude):

Nude beaches are nasty. The people you see are never the ones you want to see. And ditto, Bittersue.

From GLAMPEOPLE in Berlin, Germany:

How come there are no pictures of Count S?

From good old RINGMYBELLE in Charlotte, NC:

Good question. For all we know, he could have warts!!

Time to nip that one in the bud.

> Aside from the fact that Count S is rather surreptitious
> in general about his comings and goings, we imagine
> the paparazzi would have no trouble tracking him down
> if they really set their minds to it, despite the marquis's
> threats to go after anyone who stalks his kid with
> cameras like a pit bull. But threats like that have never
> been enough to scare away the American press. Up
> until now, it hasn't been an issue, because there hasn't
> been the demand. No one except people in France even
> knew who the count was. And who would be willing to
> pay for pictures of some unknown? But now that Count S
> is stirring things up here in the States, we imagine all
> this will change very soon and we'll be seeing plenty of
> photos of him. Hopefully we'll have them here first! As for
> the count having warts, having seen his noble visage,
> we can vehemently attest that that is not the case.

Adoringly, Mlle. Blogger

LYNN KIELE BONASIA

The no-picture thing was a problem. How long would I be able to keep this up before people lost interest? Then again, I think each Count S fan had begun to develop their own image of the guy in their mind's eye. In the same way I saw him as Spencer, they saw him as their hometown crushes, like how when you read a book, you get a general idea of how a character might look, but you fill in the rest yourself. This was really all about the noble title, and the idea of being born into position, wealth, and opportunity, all of it entirely unearned. Sure you could be a movie star heartthrob or a professional athlete, but here in America, where the playing field was supposed to be level (in theory at least), this concept of entitlement was all rather mysterious, and all the more alluring.

It was no news to me that I was living on borrowed time. If Kimmy was any example, teenage blog hounds were devastatingly fickle. I knew sooner or later this whole thing would crash and burn, whether at the hands of CELEBSTALKER19 or someone like him, or because it all just fizzled. But I wasn't ready to let things go just yet. I had an idea, a way to distract my increasingly dubious audience. A contest.

> We've been outed, friends. We suspect one of our
> informants turned on us, glammed by the count's charms,
> no doubt. In any case, S was apprised of this blog,
> and rather than demand we cease and desist, he was
> actually flattered. He sent us a private message and told
> us so himself. It was your posts, dear readers. He was
> touched by your concern. And now—are you all holding
> on to your mouses?—he has offered to meet one of his

devoted fans, and to take her out to dinner. That would
be one of you! But who? After much thought, we've all
concluded that the best way to select the most worthy
applicant would be to have a contest. So are you ready?

In fifty words or less, tell us why you should be the one
who gets to meet and have dinner with Count S.

Adoringly, Mlle. Blogger

I created a page where applicants could post their submissions.
Within seconds, I had my first.

Dear Count S,
I suffer from an overabundance of intelligence and, at the
whims of parents and teachers, have spent my entire life
cloistered away in study halls, on math clubs, and chained to
computers (as I am now). Suffice it to say I haven't gotten out
much and would give anything to hear about your world, if just
for one magical night.
NERDYGIRL from New Canaan, CT

NERDYGIRL might be a math whiz but she apparently had
difficulty counting. Her entry was ten words over the limit. Still,
I could feel her pain, that same general ennui that for me had
morphed into doldrums when the prospect that I might be something special had been dangled in front of me and then abruptly
taken away.

* * *

Friday morning, there was a nasty smell coming from the cafeteria, the kind of odor that hangs in the air for hours after lunch is served, that gets in your clothes and hair, and that you smell even when you get home. I'm guessing it was some dried herb used in the corn dog batter, though I know nothing about herbs, because my mother is a mediocre cook and Dad, while a bit better, still has a very limited repertoire. Basil. Oregano. Poultry seasoning. Bay leaves. What of chervil? Cilantro? Rosemary? Celery seed? I hadn't a clue. However, I'd always been hypersensitive to smells. The right one could make my day. The wrong one could give me a headache and make me sick to my stomach. This was what I was contemplating at the instant my two worlds collided.

Spencer and Destiny (the girl from the soup kitchen) were standing at the end of a row of lockers, beside the water fountain. I put my head down, pressed the grammar workbook I'd just picked up from my locker against my chest, and hoped to remain invisible.

"Hey, Sophie," Spencer called. "I finally remembered your yearbook." I had already given his back on Monday.

When I looked up, I saw it. At first the design just looked vaguely familiar, something about the shapes and how they were arranged. And then I realized what I was looking at. The Delorme family crest! The five-petal flowers, the ships, and the fleur-de-lis, all draped over Destiny's ample chest.

"What the heck are you looking at?" Destiny snarled. If I hadn't been so floored by the shirt, I might have picked up on her annoyance at the fact that Spencer had addressed me in the first place.

I pointed. "Where did you get *that*?"

"You mean these?" She arched her back and winked at Spencer, who looked confused. "I know. Hard to believe but they *are* real." She laughed that god-awful laugh of hers. A seal in labor.

"The shirt," I practically stammered. "That design. Where did you—"

"Sophie, what *is* it?" Spencer asked. He seemed concerned. Who could blame him, when I was pretty sure all the blood had suddenly drained from my face?

"Pretty cool, huh? It came yesterday. Found it online." Destiny tugged the shirt away from her waist so she could get a better upside-down look at the design.

"*Where?*" I practically shouted. The rest of my vocabulary had apparently vaporized.

"Oh, right, like I'm about to tell *you*, so you and all your little dweeb friends can get them and make them uncool."

"I don't *want* one," I said. I felt my nails carving moons into my palms. I shook them out and took a breath of air heavy with corn dog. My stomach lurched. "I just need to know where you got it."

"Sophie, are you okay?" Spencer asked. He flicked his hair out of his eyes. "I mean, it's just a shirt, right?"

"You'd be surprised how often I get this, Spencer. When you're a hot dresser, everyone wants to swipe your style." Destiny shook out her dark, shiny hair and swept it up into a ponytail with the elastic that had been on her wrist. "Now get lost, will you? I'm not telling you where I got the shirt and that's the end of it."

"But—"

Destiny turned on her four-inch heels. "Come on, Spencer."

"Sophie, are you sure you're okay?" he asked again.

And there it was, the answer I'd been looking for, right between Destiny's shoulder blades, in simple, unassuming gray type: celeb-stalker.com.

Someone slammed a locker and I jumped.

"Hey, Sophie," Spencer said. I took my eyes off Destiny's back. "Wait!" Spencer slid his backpack off his shoulder, unzipped it, and produced my yearbook. "At least let me give you this." He smiled.

I snatched the book out of his hands. "Thanks!" I said. I shot off down the hall.

"I signed it," I heard him call just as I was rounding the corner. The words didn't register.

That celebstalking creep. The crest. He'd swiped it off the photo I'd posted of the signet ring. No wonder he'd been so quiet this week. How in the world had he managed to print shirts so fast? And what business did he have selling our family crest?

What business did *I* have using it to make up a whole big lie about some reckless, spoiled rich kid? I felt terrible. Beyond terrible. Not only that, corn dog had permeated my sweatshirt and was making me feel like I was going to puke.

"You're awfully quiet," Mom said. She had offered to pick me up from school and drop me off at Dad's on her way to the airport. She was going to Chicago for a weeklong conference.

"Sorry. I just feel a little queasy."

Mom jumped on my words. "I can cancel my trip if you're not feeling well."

"Mom, I'm not sick," I insisted. Sam and I had finally convinced

Mom it was okay for her to leave us on our own for the weekend. Dad was just across town if we needed anything.

"I know you and Sam think this is a good idea, but I'm not so sure."

"Dad is home. We're almost sixteen. It's not a big deal. If we need something, we'll call him."

Why did I have to ask Dad to meet me at the house on this of all afternoons? I'd made the arrangement to meet him after I'd decided I really needed to talk to him about Taylor. Now all I wanted was to go back to Mom's, power up my laptop, and get to the bottom of this nightmare. Had Sam seen the shirt today? What would he think? What if Dad found out? Or the French cousins, nieces, aunts, and uncles? I'd be excommunicated from the family (if such a thing is possible), burned at the stake like Joan of Arc. What about Count S? He was the least of my problems now.

We arrived at Dad's, and Mom pulled up to the curb. I gave her a kiss and let her feel my forehead to be sure I didn't have a fever before I got out of the car. As she drove off, I saw that Dad was sitting on the porch swing, looking forlorn, as he had been recently. He stood up, and I saw he was wearing that hideous red polo shirt with the bleach stain on the belly, the one he hadn't worn in so long I thought he'd finally broken down and tossed the thing out. Only now I realized he'd kept it all along and just hadn't worn it around Taylor. Already Dad was showing signs that he was reverting to absentminded-professor mode, the way he'd been right after Mom had left. All of Taylor's good influence would be out the window in no time. Dad waved, then stuffed his hands into the pockets of his wrinkled khaki pants.

"Hey," I said when I got to the top step.

He pressed a kiss to my forehead and sniffed. "Corn dogs for lunch?" I was horrified. "So, how was your day at school?"

"Just peachy," I said.

"What's wrong?"

"Nothing." He'd made the effort to come home early and meet me. The least I could do was be civil. None of this was his fault. Then again, maybe some of it was. The count stuff, I mean. Maybe he should have fought his stuffy French ancestors, with their silly chauvinist ways. After all, this was the twenty-first century. They might have listened to him, a noble compatriot, son of a marquis, since they wouldn't listen to some snot-nosed American teen. Or he might have said to heck with all of it and taken a stand—renounced the title, sent back the ring, tossed out that old cobwebby picture of the family château. Just to be fair. I felt that pinch in my nose that told me the tears were coming.

"You okay?" Dad asked. He tilted up my chin and looked at my face. I shook his hand away and dropped my head to hide the tears, which were already making their retreat or, better yet, evaporating the second they hit my face, which had become feverish.

"Am I *okay*? How can you even ask that?" I shouted. There it was, my old pal, rage.

"Sophie, what is it?" Deep lines creased his forehead.

I couldn't tell him about the crest, or what I'd done. I couldn't tell him about Spencer, or Destiny, or Count S. I didn't truly want him to feel bad about his own heritage. I looked around the porch for something, anything, to be angry about . . . and there it was.

"It's these lights!" Even Spencer had noticed them. "I'd say

Halloween was over seven months ago, but *no*, these have actually been hanging here on this porch for four years. Since Mom left. Like this space has become a morbid symbol of our family's disgrace."

"Sophie, getting divorced is not a dis—"

"And they don't even work! We tried to plug them in last Halloween."

"All this. It cannot be about Halloween lights—"

"You don't see the broken things that are right in front of you, the things that could be fixed if you'd only make an effort."

"Did I do something to upset you? Is this about our French family—"

But now, it wasn't. "Of course not. This isn't about me. It's about you and your girlfriend, and how you're screwing up a perfectly good thing because you're frozen in the past. Because you're living like some kind of zombie. Let me ask you something, Dad. Are you actually waiting for Mom to come back?"

His faced turned red. I'd finally tripped his anger switch. "You're being ridiculous."

"*I'm* being ridiculous? You've had Taylor in your life for almost three years and you've never once introduced her to Mom. She used to practically live here, but you had her move all her stuff every time Mom came around. How do you think that makes a woman feel?" This next one was for Taylor and for me. "You need to stick up for the people you care about. You can't be so wounded that you don't take chances. You need to act on how you really feel or you'll never be happy."

Dad's anger had dissipated. His shoulders bowed forward, and I got a glimpse of the Dad who might one day greet me, my husband,

and our kids at the door on Thanksgiving a million years from now. The idea of Dad being an old man scared me a little. "Taylor loves you," I said.

Dad looked up. "Did you talk to her? Did she say that?"

"She didn't have to. What's important here is that anyone can see it. And for what it's worth, Sam and I think she's pretty great, too."

Dad ran his hand over his face. "When she left, the way it ended, I didn't think I had a chance. I thought she'd given up."

"Can you blame her? But if you really wanted to get her back, I think you could." That was it. I'd said what I'd come to say. Well, *almost*. I pointed to the bleach stain.

"What? That? It's just a bleach stain," Dad said.

"It's the color draining out of your world since Taylor left." Not bad.

Dad smiled. "You should write soap operas," he said. *Tell me about it.* "What do you say we get some ice cream, then I'll take you home?"

For that instant I had been feeling great, like maybe Dad had heard me. Then the weight of the world came crashing back down. "Can we skip the ice cream? I have a lot of homework."

"Sure," Dad said. He reached into the car for his keys. "Rain check."

A few minutes later, we were heading toward town in his beat-up tan Prius on the way back to Mom's. I knew that Spencer sometimes hung out at the TCBY where one of his teammates worked, and just prayed we'd get through town without seeing Destiny in her crest shirt. "So, school must be starting to wind down," Dad said, trying to make conversation.

"Not really. Not yet." I was distracted, already planning my CELEBSTALKER19 attack. I'd be home in three minutes. We came out from under the old railroad bridge, and that was when I saw Taylor. She was on the sidewalk in front of Starbucks.

"Hey, speak of the devil," I said. "You should swing by on your way back from dropping me off and go talk to her."

Dad looked toward the sidewalk. When he saw Taylor, he smiled. Mission accomplished, or so I thought.

Suddenly, his jaw dropped. I followed his eyes. A young guy with dark hair and sideburns peeking out from under his knit cap finished putting quarters in the parking meter, then came around and gave Taylor a hug. She nuzzled her face into his neck, then broke away. They moved toward the Starbucks hand in hand.

Dad's eyes were back on the road, his brow furrowed.

"Maybe it's her brother."

"Look, Sophie, let's just forget about it, okay?" he said. "And for the record, she doesn't have a brother." After stopping for an old lady in the crosswalk, Dad stepped on the gas a little too hard. My head flew back into the seat rest.

I was about to suggest that maybe he was just some guy from yoga class, but then decided not to say anything. For all I knew, he was some guy from yoga class who had just replaced Dad.

When I got inside the condo, I heard Dad peel away from the front of the house, which confirmed, once again, how upset he was. Dad had never been a "peeler."

The condo was dark. I flicked on a light and Sam appeared in the hallway.

"*Where* have you *been?*" He shifted his weight to one leg and put his hands on his hips.

"Oh, excuse me. I guess you've signed on for Mom's job while she's gone?" I thought it was funny, even if he didn't crack a smile. "I was at Dad's, talking to him about Taylor, remember?" I tried to barrel past, pinning Sam to the wall with my backpack.

"Sophie, *wait!*"

I swung around. "What?"

"You're not going to believe what I saw at school today," he said. Crap. Based on his general cluelessness about women's clothes, I hoped there'd be a chance he wouldn't have noticed.

"Let me guess. A bimbo wearing a shirt with our family crest on it," I said.

"Huh? No. It was on some freshman's backpack. You saw it on a *shirt?*" Sam slapped his forehead with his palm. "Sophie, what's up with that? You think some French relative is trying to cash in on the family stuff? We should tell Dad—"

A *backpack?*

"No, we can't tell Dad," I said. *Think quick, Sophie.* "We need to get our facts straight. Let me ask around and do a little research."

"But Dad should tell the family. They might have lawyers for this kind of thing," Sam said.

Oh, great. "Look, I didn't want to get into this with you now, but something happened a few minutes ago. I already told you I went over to Dad's to talk to him about Taylor, and by the end of it, I really thought I'd gotten through to him. But then when he was taking me home, we saw Taylor with some guy."

"Where? What guy?"

"They were going into Starbucks. They hugged in kind of an intimate way and Dad saw. He was pretty upset."

"Jeez." Sam shook his head.

"So I think the last thing he needs is more drama, right? We just need to give him some time."

"But—"

"Look, I've got homework and I want to talk to Kimmy." I took a few steps toward my room. Sam remained in his doorway. "I'll let you know if I hear anything else. Leave it to me, okay?"

"Okay," he said. I could tell he was thinking about Dad and not the crest anymore.

> Dear Count S,
> You're a man, and based on my experience, all men are . . .
> how do you say . . . cochons. Then again, just maybe you're
> a decent guy and can restore my faith, if not in American
> men, then perhaps their European counterparts. The future of
> hommekind rests in your hands.
> BITTERSUE from Nantucket, MA
>
> Dear Count S,
> Have you ever considered switching teams? The best part
> about dating a guy like me is that I'll never complain when you
> want to watch football. Or is it le football? And the toilet seat
> stays up. Always. Think about it.
> QUEENBEE from Fire Island, NY

Finally in my room, I fired up my laptop and saw the deluge of contest entries. For a moment, I allowed myself to revel in the fact that I'd managed to generate such excitement. I clicked through the first few dozen entries, forgetting what I'd rushed in here to do. Young girls from all over the world were laying bare their souls for a chance to have dinner with my Frankenstein. Truly, I'd created a monster. With that thought, naturally CELEBSTALKER19 came to mind. I went to his Web site and there, in the top corner where the notes about Count S's comings and goings had been featured, sat a big, fat black-and-gold crest, and underneath it: *Visit our store.* The landing page had a headline that said *How do we love thee? Let us "count" the ways.* And some text: *Show the world you're a fan of the biggest European hottie to cross the pond since Jude Law.* (Hey! That was my line!) *It's Count S's authentic family crest, available for a limited time. Vive la France!*

Beneath the copy were boxes featuring ridiculously overpriced merchandise: T-shirts, tank tops, backpacks, mouse pads, coffee mugs, baseball caps, and (worst of all!) Delorme family crest boxer *underwear*, which, to my horror, had apparently sold out. I thought I might die. All this had been my doing, albeit indirectly. But I'd prostituted my own family crest to inflate my ego. And even worse, this opportunist creep was profiting from it.

My noble blood pressure rose to a dangerous level. I clicked on the "Contact us" button, which opened up an e-mail with *CELEBSTALKER19* in the recipient window. Into the subject window, I typed:

WHAT DO YOU THINK YOU'RE DOING??!!

CHAPTER SEVEN

· ·

Dear Count S,

I have a thing for vampires and I'm thinking maybe you're
one. Let's discuss it over dinner, though vampires don't eat
food, do they? Not to worry, your secret's safe with me. As for
the rest of you nonbelievers, bite me.

GOTHGIRL from North Conway, NH

"Sophie, get your butt down here!" Sam called from the kitchen.
Having survived our unsupervised weekend, we were now back
at Dad's, though it was finals week and Dad had left early for
campus.

"I'm coming!" I had meant to get up early so I could check
to see if I'd gotten any response from CELEBSTALKER19, but
I'd had a lousy night's sleep and had only just fallen into a deep
snooze minutes before the alarm went off. Now I was scrambling
to get dressed and do a quick check before I had to go. There
were hundreds more contest entries, including one from a self-
proclaimed vampire. But not a peep from CELEBSTALKER19. He

was probably too busy counting the money he was making off our family.

I looked over at Sam, whose head was buried in his cereal bowl, which was sitting in his upside-down Frisbee. I examined Sam like he was a science project. *"Really?"* I said. I poured myself some cereal, slid into my chair, and grabbed for the milk.

"I knew you were going to say something. But it's technically mine, or it will be someday, so why can't I wear it?"

"Huh? I was talking about eating out of a Frisbee. Who *does* that?" Then I saw what he was referring to: the family signet ring on his index finger. "Sam! You're just as bad as the rest of them."

"No, I'm not. I'm the only one who *should* wear it."

"Rub it in," I said.

Sam dropped the spoon into his cereal bowl. "Look. People are just starting to think I'm cool. Give me a break."

He had a point, I supposed. I already established being popular isn't easy. "Just don't lose it or Dad will kill you," I said. "Frankly, I'm surprised he even let you have it in the first place."

Sam had the bowl to his lips and was guzzling down milk. His Adam's apple looked like a cat playing under the sheets.

I got about three spoonfuls of cereal into my mouth before I realized we had to leave or we'd miss the bus. "Sam, let's go!"

The gap between first and second periods was the only time other than afternoon study hall when Kimmy's and my schedules synched up so that we could see each other. Though we were in different classes, we both had language in the same wing. Right now, the one morning I desperately needed to talk to her, she was nowhere to be found, which would not be so dire had her parents not chosen this past weekend for an impromptu family trip to Rhode Island to visit Grandma. I hadn't talked to her since Friday morning. Since everything had changed.

Maybe her social studies teacher had asked her to erase the boards again. She was always too nice to say no. I stood with my back to the lockers outside her classroom door, hoping she'd appear before the first bell.

"Hey," I heard. I turned around. It was Spencer. Normally, I'd have been beside myself, but I'd made up my mind that morning that I was going to tell Kimmy everything, so my head was swimming with practice sentences.

"Hi," I managed.

"Sorry for the way Destiny treated you on Friday. That wasn't cool." He looked down and mashed his toe into the bottom of the nearest locker.

I looked over Spencer's shoulder, thinking it was Kimmy's pink sweatshirt I saw in the crowd. It wasn't. "No problem. I'm sure it seemed weird of me to make such a big deal about a shirt. I had my reasons."

"Yeah, well, if it's any consolation, I told Destiny to take a hike," he said. He flipped his hair out of his eyes. After seeing him with the cheerleader in the parking lot, I'd assumed he was probably done with Destiny anyway. Then he added, "Did you get a chance to see what I wrote in your yearbook?"

Oh my God, I had completely forgotten. Spencer had signed my yearbook and given it back to me, and I hadn't even looked to see what he'd written. I needed to have my head examined. What's worse, I'd left the book in Mom's car on Friday when she'd picked me up at school, which meant the yearbook would be sitting at the Logan Airport parking lot until she got back from her trip. Just then Kimmy appeared through the double doors as the first bell rang. "Kimmy!" I hollered.

I turned to Spencer and for some reason I'll never understand, I lied to him. "Yeah, loved what you wrote. Really clever. Thanks a lot. Hey, I desperately need to talk to Kimmy. I'll catch you in class, okay?" Then I bolted toward my best friend without looking back. She seemed to be heading my way at an equal velocity.

"Tutoring in the halls now?" she teased before I had a chance to speak. "What did he say? Oh, tell me later. Listen, where did your brother get that ring?"

"Huh?"

"Don't you read your e-mail? I sent you a link. There's this blog I was trying to tell you about last weekend. It tracks all the fringe celebs, including this hot count kid who's supposedly here in New England, or at least he was. Anyway, the stuff they sell is totally hot and this past week it's been this kid's family crest, which of course no one would know about unless they're cool enough to follow the site. I saw everything they were selling, which was all ridiculously expensive, and there was no jewelry. I'm sure of it. So where did he—"

That instant the second bell rang. We were late.

"I'll see you during study hall. I have something to tell you." Then we both flew to our classes. But leave it to Kimmy to have been the one to find out about my count. If she knew about it, then pretty soon everyone would.

> *Cher Comte S,*
> *Salut, j'habite dans les environs de Paris et n'ai jamais*
> *entendu parler de vous. Est-ce possible? Quittez ces*
> *impudentes Américaines et revenez en France. J'espère que*
> *vous ferez preuve de bon sens avant qu'il ne soit trop tard.*
> *Choisissez moi!*
> *LACOQUETTE en Rueil-Malmaison, FR*

[My attempt at a translation: Hello. I live outside Paris and have never heard of you! How can that be? Leave these nasty American women alone and come home to France. I hope you come to your senses before it's too late. Choose me!]

> *Dear Count S,*
> *I sit here in your family crest T-shirt, cap, and boxers (ooh la*
> *la), sipping tea from your family crest mug, navigating over*
> *your family crest mouse pad, your family crest backpack at my*
> *feet. If that's not devotion, I don't know what is.*
> *MORTGAGINGTHECAT in Des Moines, IA*

I got out of chemistry early and had the chance to snag one of the library computers, where I could log on and check e-mail from my Web site. A hundred more contest entries but no word from CELEBSTALKER19, so I decided to write a brief post.

> Thanks so much for all the wonderful entries, which we
> continue to forward on to our beloved count. On a bit of
> a sour note, Count S has just gotten wind that someone
> here in the States has been selling unauthorized

merchandise emblazoned with his family crest. While he's humbled by everyone's enthusiasm, he fears the wrath that may befall the purveyor should the marquis (who already has his knickers in a twist, thanks to the recent defection of his wife) find out. The count suggests to his fans that they spend their money on good French chocolate rather than this gauche attire, and further implores this Celebstalker to knock it off. But don't take our word for it. The legal hounds have been unleashed.

Adoringly, Mlle. Blogger

I checked my e-mail from the site one more time. CELEB-STALKER19 had responded to my WHAT DO YOU THINK YOU'RE DOING??!! message. His reply: *Selling stuff.*

I wrote: What gives you the right to sell stuff with the count's family crest on it?

Within a minute, a response came. *That might be a problem if there actually was a count.*

My heart skipped a beat. I typed: What do you mean?! Of course there's a count. (After all, I almost had myself convinced.)

Another instantaneous response: *You made him up. And I was clever enough to cash in. Trust me, in another week this will all be yesterday's news.*

I replied: How did you even get the stuff made up so fast?

He answered: *How do they have Super Bowl victory shirts printed overnight? I have people.*

I wrote: You're wrong, you know. There is a count. And he's not happy about any of this.

I waited for a response but none came. I was furious. How could he (if he was indeed a "he") be so sure of himself? How had this guy been able to see through my story from the beginning?

"Whatcha doin'?" Kimmy appeared behind me just as I closed the e-mail window. My hands were shaking.

"You'd better sit down."

There, hidden behind a rack of dusty books, I told her about the family title and my own rotten luck, and about Sam's ring. I told her about the fake blog I'd started after talking with Taylor about writing. I told her about the overwhelming public response and how this CELEBSTALKER19 parasite had posed as a dubious fan and then cashed in by selling merchandise, which I'd seen Destiny sporting. I told her about my most recent CELEBSTALKER19 e-mail exchange. Then Kimmy said she'd actually been following my blog, and proceeded to tell me about the other kids she'd seen wearing the paraphernalia—all popular kids. If this whole thing hadn't become so traumatic, I might have even been amused. Oh, the irony! I wondered if corporate marketing bigwigs were actually once nerdy kids like me and got a charge out of seeing their lifelong tormenters (the "in" crowd) open their wallets and jump through hoops to get whatever they were selling.

"Oh, and one more thing," I said.

Kimmy, who had chewed her pen cap to a pulp over the course of my confession, looked up. "What?"

"Actually, make that three more things," I said.

Kimmy raised her eyebrows.

"Dad and I saw Taylor hugging another guy in front of the Starbucks yesterday. He was young and pretty good-looking. This after I had practically convinced Dad that Taylor still loved him."

"Wow, that was fast on her part."

"Tell me about it." The study period was almost over. Kimmy and I started packing up the books we'd set out to look like we'd actually been working.

"The other thing is that I lied to Spencer. I told him I liked what he wrote in my yearbook, but I haven't actually read it yet."

"You what? Why would you do a thing like—"

"Because I had no excuse for not reading it, at least no excuse that I could let him in on. And then I knew I left it in Mom's car and wouldn't be able to read it until she got back. So I just said I liked it."

"And what did he say?"

"I didn't stick around long enough to find out," I said.

"Sophie! Now I'm afraid to ask. What's the other thing?"

"I started this contest on the blog." I stuffed my science binder into my backpack. I could feel Kimmy's eyes on me, but I didn't look up.

"Oh my God, that's right, you did! I saw it this morning!" Kimmy fanned her face with her Spanish notebook. Papers flew out. "What were you *thinking*?"

"Fans were getting impatient over the blog's lack of photos, so I needed a way to deflect attention."

"This has been a real head trip for you, hasn't it?" Kimmy said. I could avoid her gaze no longer. "I'll admit it's pretty impressive, how you managed to break through so fast. But you're lying to people, and you'd better be careful." She tried to stick her history textbook into her already overstuffed backpack. It wasn't fitting. "What's the prize?"

"Dinner with Count S?" It came out like a question.

Kimmy dropped the book on the table. The librarian shot us a nasty look, accompanied by a *shhhh*. "Are you out of your mind?"

"Relax." I tried to reassure her, though my voice cracked. I started chewing on the drawstring of my sweatshirt. "At least no one is asking for pictures anymore."

Kimmy rested her hands on her hips. She lifted her chin, like she always does when she's trying to convince me she's right about something. "Sophie, what do you intend to do about the winner? I mean, somebody's gotta win, right?"

I looked down at the table, which was carved up with initials. I couldn't even imagine the time it would take to read through all those entries. "I thought I'd worry about that when the time comes."

"Well, you realize there's only one way out of this," she said. The resolve in her voice scared me a little. Whatever it was, I knew it wouldn't be good.

"What do you mean?"

"You have to rig it so *you* win."

"*Me?*"

Kimmy folded her arms, then tapped her finger on her cheek. "We'll have to announce a location and get a guy." She opened up a side pocket of her backpack and managed to stuff the textbook into it, though she couldn't zip the zipper.

I was just trying to process it all. "A *guy*?"

"Someone to pose as Count S for a photo op. Someone who then just disappears forever." Kimmy wrestled with her zipper. "Or you're toast."

"Why can't I just shut the whole thing down right before I announce the winner?" I admit, even saying that made me a little sad.

"You said that Celebstalker guy is on to the fact that you're a fake."

"So?"

Kimmy dropped her backpack on the floor and sat back down. I followed her lead, even though I knew the bell would be ringing any second. "Right now he has no reason to expose you because he's making money off your family crest. But if you suddenly shut down, people who've been following both sites, including people from around here, will want to know what's up. If they think the whole thing was a scam, that'll tarnish his reputation. Who'll buy his stuff after that? Keep in mind that being in the know is what he's all about."

"How does he even know I'm a fake?"

"I suspect he's good at spotting sites that are getting a little buzz, and then figuring out that the mastermind behind them is some bored teen who should be saving her short story writing for English class." *Oh, snap.*

"Come on, Kimmy."

"I'm guessing it doesn't really matter whether the gossip is true or not, as long as he can find a way to repackage it and make money off of it." How did Kimmy get so savvy all of a sudden?

She continued. "Whether or not the count ever existed probably doesn't even matter to him. That is, until his reputation takes a hit. Then, I suspect he'd do whatever he can to save his skin, even if it means wrecking the life of some teenage kid by exposing her to the world."

I felt a chill run up my spine. "I'd be social toast from Putnam to Paris." But wait. Maybe Kimmy wasn't so savvy after all. "But how could he ever trace it back to me?"

Finally, the first bell rang. Kimmy got up. I followed.

"You gave him the crest, right? And he knows you're in the Boston area. He could try tracing the coat of arms and then matching it to last names in greater Boston. How many Delormes can there be?" Kimmy slung the backpack over her shoulder. "If he's as shameless as we suspect he is, trust me, there are plenty of ways he could find out."

Kimmy started for the door. There were kids around, so she lowered her voice. "When people around here find out you've won the contest, you're going to be the most popular kid in school."

"That's never been my goal."

"You wanted to know what it felt like to be something special, right?" Kimmy pushed open the library door. "Now you will."

In a minute we'd be heading in different directions. I stopped and pinned her against the wall. "How about if we rig it so *you* win?" I pleaded.

"Nice try. But counts aren't my type."

How could I argue with her? This was my doing. I had to take the rap.

"I'll see you later," Kimmy said. Then, over her shoulder, "Don't worry, we'll figure it out."

As we started for our last classes of the day, I felt a pang of fear. "Kimmy?" I called. She turned around. "It'll be okay, right?" I said.

She gave me a halfhearted thumbs-up.

After school, I went straight to Dad's. Sam had Frisbee and wouldn't be home until later. How had I gotten myself into such a mess? The chance that Kimmy and I could pull any of this off without being found out seemed infinitesimal. Kimmy. Thank God for her. She'd thought of so many things I hadn't. I was too caught up in my power trip. My fatal mistake was failing to realize that fiction wasn't fiction unless other people knew it was.

I walked to my room, dumped my backpack on the floor, and flopped onto my bed. The first order of business was announcing a date for the contest winner to be chosen. The second, of course, was finding a guy. But who? It couldn't be Sam (ew!) or anyone from school. He had to be someone who couldn't be easily traced. And of course, he had to be handsome and speak French, or at least be able to fake an accent well. And he needed to be willing to go along with this whole ridiculous scheme. Why would any guy in his right mind be willing to do that?

Speaking of guys, I grabbed the phone in my room and dialed Taylor's number. I just couldn't wrap my brain around how she could have replaced Dad so fast. No matter how bad it looked, none of it made sense. I had to give her the benefit of the doubt. The phone rang and then her voice mail picked up.

Hi. This is Taylor. Sorry I missed you. Please leave a message. Namaste.

"Taylor, it's Sophie. I don't know if you've talked to Dad, but I wanted to give you the heads-up. We saw you with that guy in front of Starbucks. Dad was driving me home. He was pretty bent out of shape . . . actually more hurt, I think. I guess that's it. . . . Except that I hope you haven't given up on Dad and found someone else. I mean, I understand if you did, but . . . oh crap, forget it. Bye."

Wow. Could I have sounded any more desperate? Dad would be better off fighting his own battles.

I logged back on to my site e-mail, where I found another message from CELEBSTALKER19.

> *I noticed your little post about the illegitimacy of my merchandise. I'm afraid I'm going to have to ask you to retract. Bad for business. You understand.*

I responded: What if I don't?

In a matter of seconds, this appeared: *Then everyone finds out that your dear countie is a fake, you get exposed, and my guess is you'll have real trouble finding a date for the prom.*

Kimmy was right. This guy was soulless. Why do I think you're not nineteen? I wrote.

Then came the reply: *I'm forty-three, doll.*

> *Dear Count S,*
> *I'm the one who told you I bought all your crest stuff. You'll be happy to know I'm now in the buff, toasting marshmallows*

*over a roaring fire fueled by ill-gotten merchandise. And
wishing you were here. And for the record, plastic coffee
mugs and mouse pads don't burn. They melt.
MORTGAGINGTHECAT in Des Moines, IA*

I blogged:

Guess we were a little hasty on that family crest
merchandise post. It turns out one of our informants
spotted Count S sporting the long-sleeved tee from the
offender's collection. Apparently no one is immune to
count mania, not even our dear S. I must say, I rather like
the stuff myself, and may have to pick up a T-shirt or two.

Adoringly, Mlle. Blogger

I gagged writing that last comment, but what choice did I have?
I had become slave to a forty-three-year-old paparazzi extortionist.
And to top it off, the whole thing was my own doing.

CHAPTER EIGHT

• •

Okay. I get it. This is a test. Well, I just reordered all the stuff I burned, and it should be arriving any day now. At least, I hope it's a test. Because I'm already late on this month's rent. But if this is how I prove my devotion, I'm willing to do whatever it takes.
MORTGAGINGTHECAT in Des Moines, IA

That one got to me. I was messing with people's lives. I was giving them hope for a knight in shining armor who didn't even exist. I needed to end this, whether I was ready to or not.

The date was set. Two weeks from today, a winner—me—would be announced. Days later, I'd be meeting Count S at an undisclosed location for a romantic dinner.

And I was probably as terrified as I would have been if I were actually meeting a handsome count, but obviously for a whole different set of reasons. Among them, the fact that there was no count.

As I heard the late bus pull up, I looked up from my laptop. From my window at Dad's, I saw Sam get off. His head was down. There was something wrong, I could tell. The Esses and our "twintuition." I hadn't been a very good sister lately, lying to him, blaming him for stuff that he had no control over, and being too wrapped up in my own drama to care about what was going on in his life. What if he hadn't made the Frisbee team? What if Michelle had broken his heart?

When we were little kids, we were inseparable. And then that first day of kindergarten came, and they put us in different classrooms. I felt like someone had ripped out one of my organs. Mom says we were pretty upset at the time. Even the teachers were worried about us. And then something happened that helped us both make a move toward independence. Ironically, it involved another set of twins—identicals. Sam and I had never seen identical twins before, so it came as quite a shock when I got on the school bus one morning and saw two little boys with the same face. Sam still tells the story of how I slid into the seat in front of them, then turned and stared at them the entire ride. Finally, as the bus rolled into the school drop-off area, I said, "So which one of you stole the other one's face?" Before they even had a chance to answer (and I'm not sure what answer they could possibly have given), I whipped around and smacked Sam on the arm.

"Ouch!" he'd hollered. "What was that for?"

"Don't you *ever* steal my face."

"Huh?"

"Look!" I'd said. I pointed to the identical twins. Sam got up and looked, then sat back down. He didn't say anything, just rubbed his arm. To this day he denies that seeing the identical twins rattled him, but I know it did.

In the days that followed, I'd been afraid to be around Sam, because I was sure that he had secret twin-face-stealing powers. Being on my own helped me focus on meeting new kids and learning the alphabet. As for Sam, whether it was fear of having his face stolen or of being smacked by his sister, he was more comfortable being on his own, too. By the time we forgot about the twin incident, or perhaps had the situation explained to us rationally by a patient adult, we had become two separate and independent living, breathing organisms, to the extent that that was possible.

Now I heard my fellow organism head up to his room and close his door. Drawers opened, then slammed shut, and then the closet door was practically ripped off its hinges. Something crashed to the floor. Enough was enough. I got up from my desk, walked down the hall, and knocked on Sam's door.

"Go away!" my brother shouted.

Naturally, I took that as my cue to open the door. "What the heck is going on?" I asked.

"Do you not understand English?" Sam threw his backpack on his bed.

"*Non, je parle seulement francais.*"

"Not funny." He unzipped the zipper and emptied the backpack's contents onto his comforter. Books, notebooks, pen caps, gum wrappers, a broken protractor, a few rogue Frito crumbs, a condom. A *what*?

Once I caught my breath, I hollered: "Samuel Delorme! Are you having . . . ?"

He looked down on the bed, saw the foil packet, picked it up, and flicked it at me. "*Please.*"

I ducked as the flying square whizzed past my ear. "Well then, where did you get *that*?" I asked.

"They passed them out in health class. Do you mind? I'm kind of busy here." He unzipped a side pocket and thrust his hand inside.

"What are you looking for?" I asked. And then it hit me. I swallowed. "Sam, you didn't lose the ring."

"I had it on before gym class. And then I took it off because it was kind of loose, and I swear I put it in my backpack for safekeeping. Inside this bag." He turned the Frito bag upside down. Gold crumbs fell onto the bed.

"YOU PUT THE PRIZED FAMILY SIGNET RING INSIDE A PIECE OF TRASH FOR SAFEKEEPING?"

"You're not helping!"

"Oh my God." I started pacing. "Dad is going to kill you!"

"Ya think? Either help me look for it, or get lost," Sam said.

Sam and I spent the next two hours mentally retracing his steps. We searched his entire room, the house, the yard. We turned his backpack inside out, then repeated the whole process again. No ring. It was gone.

That night Sam didn't come down for dinner. He couldn't look Dad in the eye. Dad asked what was up with him, and I said there was a bug going around at school. After dinner, I brought Sam a tray of food. I knocked on the door. "Get lost!" he yelled. This time, I cut him some slack and left the tray on the floor by the door. He really did sound sick. He had lost our father's prized ring. And it was all my fault for posting the crest online in the first place. How much worse could this get?

I was enjoying a good catatonic stare into my lava lamp when my phone rang. I looked at the caller ID and saw that it was Taylor. I took a deep breath.

"Hello," I said.

"Sophie. It's Taylor."

"I know."

"I only just got your message from last week. Honestly, Sophie. Do you really think I could move on from your father that fast?"

"I don't know what to think," I said.

"And the idea that *he* could think that . . ." She trailed off.

I felt a little defensive on Dad's behalf. So what if we were a wounded bunch? "We saw what we saw, Taylor."

"That *guy* you're referring to is my cousin, Kardos. He's visiting from Hungary, and I hadn't seen him in almost five years."

I didn't know what to say. I felt enormously stupid. "I feel enormously stupid," I said. "I'm sorry. I shouldn't have assumed," I added. "It's just been a rough week." My voice cracked a little.

"What is it, Sophie? Something's wrong, I can tell."

I sighed. "How much time do you have?"

"All the time you need. You know that. I'm always here for you."

That sort of opened the floodgates. "Taylor, I'm in big trouble." And then I told her everything. I justified telling her because she was the one who'd suggested I start writing in the first place. Of course I couldn't blame her for what I'd written or how I'd chosen to do it. But she was clearly a creative person, and it was going to take some serious creativity to get me out of the bind I was in.

Sure enough, after I poured out my heart, Taylor said, "I have an idea. But you'll have to move the whole thing up a week."

*　　*　　*

For Taylor's plan to work, I had to announce the winner of the contest this Friday at the very latest. Fortunately, when I called Kimmy and told her about Taylor's idea, she was totally on board. Now we just needed to nail down the details. But first I needed to straighten Dad out about what we'd seen in front of Starbucks the other day.

I went downstairs in the I ❤ ME pajamas Taylor had given me the past Christmas (a little cloying, but considering most teen-age girls suffer from some form of self-loathing, not a bad affirmation). It was almost nine. Sam was still upstairs as far as I knew, and Dad was in the living room, grading student papers. He was in his favorite chair, a glass of cognac resting on top of a pile of science-fiction library books on the coffee table.

"Boy, are you going to feel silly when you hear this," I said. I plopped myself down onto the sofa across from him and tucked my feet up underneath me.

"What's that, hon?" Dad slid his glasses down his nose. I thought he looked sad, like someone who'd just found out his dog didn't like him.

"I talked to Taylor tonight."

Dad took off his reading glasses. "You did *what?*"

"Rather than stew about it, I just wanted some answers."

Dad rubbed the bridge of his nose. "I appreciate that, but don't you think I can manage my own—"

"No. Because after seeing Taylor and that guy, you were practically running little old ladies off the road." I twisted my hair into a knot at the base of my neck. "But it turns out Taylor's actions were completely legit. That guy is her cousin from Hungary."

"I didn't know she had a—"

"Precisely. I didn't, either. So we talked about it, and she told me. And I believe her. End of story."

Sam burst through the front door. I heard a car pull away. From the porch, through the sheer curtains, he must have seen me on the sofa—though he obviously hadn't seen Dad.

"I got it back! Thanks to Michelle. It must've fallen out of the chip bag and somehow ended up on the field and she—" Sam stopped when he saw Dad.

But that didn't make sense. He said the chip bag had been inside his backpack.

"What's going on?" Dad asked. "What did you lose?"

"You mean *find*," I said, correcting him.

Sam's face blanched. He looked at me, wide-eyed, then at Dad. "Nothing. Everything's great now. Gotta go finish my homework." Sam made a start for the stairs.

"Hang on a minute. I'd like to know what's going on," Dad said in his "dad" voice.

Sam's shoulders slumped a little. He was going to cave, I could tell. He was a horrible liar. "I just brought the family crest ring to school, and then it—"

"You did *what*? Without even *asking*?" Dad shouted.

So he hadn't even asked! This could get ugly. I needed to intervene. "It was for French class," I said. "For the kids going to Montreal. They had to do it in my class, too, an extra assignment where they had to bring something French in and talk about it. In French, of course. Sam was telling me about the look on Madame Phippen's face when she saw the ring. She obviously knew how significant it was." Sam looked at me and nodded as if to say "what she said." "Of course, ever the considerate brother, he didn't tell her what it all meant."

"Sam, you should have asked. This is an important piece of our family history. Not something to be left in a chip bag or on a field." Dad shook his head. "A chip bag!"

"I'm sorry, Dad. It was irresponsible of me, I know." Sam hung his head.

"Do you have the ring now?" Dad asked.

"Yeah."

"Would you please give it to me?" Dad held out his hand. "I'll hang on to it for safekeeping until you're old enough and careful enough to take care of it."

Sam didn't argue. He reached into his pocket and dropped the ring into Dad's palm. While Dad inspected it, we held our breath. Finally, he slipped it onto his right index finger. At that moment I felt unfathomable relief, like just maybe everything was going to be okay after all. Though the minute I had that thought, I realized I might have just jinxed myself.

Thursday morning I met Kimmy at our usual place by the lockers outside French class.

"So tomorrow's the big day," she said. "You've got to post yourself as the winner tonight."

"I know. I'm a little nervous."

"I don't blame you. This time tomorrow, you'll be the coolest kid in school. Wonder what that feels like." Kimmy's eyes glazed over a little.

"Watch out what you wish for," I said. Not that I'd ever actually wished to be the most popular kid in school. Being noticed would have been enough.

Just then Destiny and her entourage of fashionistas, at least one of whom was festooned with a family crest, walked by. Spencer was passing by in the other direction on his way to French class. Destiny tried to catch Spencer's eye, but he didn't look at her. So he had meant it when he'd told her to take a hike. I felt some sense of satisfaction until he ignored Kimmy and me as well, walking right by us without so much as looking up. Then I remembered my yearbook lie. I must've blown it.

"By the way, did Sam get his ring back?" Kimmy asked.

"Huh?" I watched Spencer until he disappeared into the classroom. Apparently, he hated me now. And I had no idea why. Then what Kimmy had said finally registered. I turned to her. "How did you know it was missing?"

"I heard it from Sarah Faulkner, who heard it from Kitty Davis, that Michelle Alberghetti showed up wearing it to the student council dinner last night."

"When was that?" I asked.

"I don't know, around seven. It was at Denny's. Can you believe that?" Kimmy wrinkled her nose. "*Denny's?* And these are people we've elected to represent us?"

Michelle Alberghetti, that liar. She must have taken it from him at Frisbee, intending to wear it that night. At least she'd given it back, but still . . . The bell rang.

"I heard one of the cheerleaders dared her to swipe it," Kimmy added. She lifted her backpack and slung it over her shoulder.

Sam was so clueless. "She dropped it off at the house last night, obviously after the dinner," I said. Now the question was, should I tell Sam or should I not tell Sam?

And the other question: was Spencer actually mad at me for not reading what he'd written in my yearbook? And if so, what the heck did he write? And how would I survive without knowing until Mom came home on Sunday?

Ladies and gents (because we know for a fact that there are more than few of you gents out there):

The long-awaited day has arrived. Count S wants to be sure we pass along how grateful he is for all your entries. He said (in his adorable accent) that he was extremely flattered by "ze" outpouring of affection.

So without further ado, we'd like to announce the winner of the Dinner with Count S Contest. After much deliberation, it was decided by a panel of expert judges (that would be us and Count S) that our beloved S will be having dinner with . . . drumroll, please . . . **Sophie Delorme from Putnam, Massachusetts.** The pair will meet at an undisclosed location this coming Tuesday. And of course, we will be on hand to report every detail. And take pictures.

So, no tears. And thank you for all your wonderful, clever, thoughtful, inspiring entries. À bientôt!

Adoringly, Mlle. Blogger

The responses to my post came rushing in almost immediately and ranged from messages congratulating Sophie to bitter rants. Most notable was this from my dear old pal:

> Tomorrow at 8 A.M.: SOPHIE, HOW DO I HATE THEE? LET ME
> **COUNT** THE WAYS T-shirts will be available on celebstalker.com.
> They come in all colors and sizes.
> —CELEBSTALKER19

Like they say, as soon as you make it to the top, there's someone trying to knock you back down.

Within minutes, Kimmy called. She'd seen the announcement post.

"What are you going to wear tomorrow?" she asked.

CHAPTER NINE

● ● ● ● ● ● ● ● ● ● ● ● ● ● ● ● ● ● ● ●

I felt the eyeballs on me, burning holes into my being. Little beams of energy piercing my flesh. I felt naked. I made it past the cafeteria, chemistry binder pressed to my chest, and finally dared to look up. Toby Finch, the most clueless kid in school, was sitting on the bench outside the main office, scraping gum off his shoe with a bottle cap.

"What the heck are you looking at?" he barked at me.

Okay, so Toby Finch was still the most clueless kid in school.

"Hey, congratulations!" I whipped around. It was Sarah Faulkner, one of those girls notorious for giving you the time of day only if no one more important was around.

"Thanks," I said. There it was. The first one out of the way. It wasn't so bad.

One of the freshmen I knew from track seemed to pop out of a locker. "Sophie, can you believe it? You must be so excited!" She started walking backward in front of me.

"Yeah, thanks." I felt like I was in a musical, as if at any moment someone might burst into song.

"Oh my God, I'd kill to be you," she said. Her sneaker caught a crack in the tile, and she spun back around to catch her balance. "I want to know what you wrote. I mean, what did you *say* to him?"

"Um. Well, I—" My face got hot.

"Hey. You dressed the part." Kimmy had managed to come up alongside me without my even knowing it, rescuing me from the freshman. I was grateful to see an ally. "You look nice."

"Thanks."

Last night before bed, I had laid out what I was going to wear. After rejecting just about every top I owned, I dug deep, producing a belted navy blue Urban Outfitters shirtdress with the tags still on, black tights, and combat boots. This morning, I'd changed my mind another three or four times, finally settling on a black mini Mom had bought me at the beginning of the school year (which I'd hated until I saw that all the cool girls had the same skirt), green-and-black argyle tights, and a green cardigan over a ruffled white top. This was a big departure from my usual T-shirts and jean skirts. I had even thrown on a long strand of shell beads for the heck of it.

"Sophie, don't you look pretty?" Dad had said earlier. When I had come down for breakfast, he was still in his pajamas, leaning against the stove with the Sports section in his hands.

"Thanks," I said. "Did you call Taylor yet?"

"I will today." He folded the paper and tucked it under his arm, then kissed me on the forehead and headed upstairs to get ready for work.

I heard an avalanche of feet coming down the stairs. "See you later, Pop," Sam said as he passed Dad on the steps. How could two feet manage to sound like twenty?

When Sam saw me, he came to a dead stop. "Track season's over, right?" he asked. I guess he assumed I was dressed for an away meet.

"Yeah."

"What's with the costume?" Sam reached around me, grabbed a triangle of buttered raisin toast, and shoved the whole thing into his mouth. I watched the hinge of his jaw pop as he struggled to close his mouth.

"Gee, thanks." To be honest, it did feel a bit like a costume.

"You look good," Sam said, spitting crumbs, "much as it pains me to say it."

He could be so gross. Somehow, the refinement of my attire made me more appalled at his behavior than usual. "Why do you *do* that?"

"'Cause I can," he said, smirking.

I had to duck to avoid a flying raisin. "Listen," I said. Sam reached for another piece of toast, and I slapped his hand away. Lowering my voice, I continued. "I helped you out the other night. You know, when I covered for you with Dad about why you brought the ring to school."

Sam swallowed. "French class. That was impressive," he said.

"So you *owe* me."

"Uh-oh, here it comes." Sam folded his arms.

"There's something that's going to be going on at school today. It involves that family crest stuff you've been seeing around—"

"Yeah, I heard about some Web site and figured you knew more than you were—"

"There's this contest that I won." I didn't like lying to Sam's face, so I turned around and took a piece of toast. I nibbled on a corner.

"What contest? What did you win?"

"A date with a count." A piece of toast got stuck in my dry throat and I coughed. "It was announced last night. It's going to be all around school."

"A count? What? Announced *where*?" By the look on Sam's face, I could tell he was worried he was somehow going to be roped into going on a date with his sister.

"Not you, dweeb. *Another* count."

Sam thought for a moment. "This sounds a little too convenient—"

I turned to the sink to pour a glass of water. "I know, right? What are the odds?"

"Sophie!" I felt a hand on my forearm. I jerked it free. "Be straight with me for once. Does this have to do with the stuff with our family crest on it? What did you do?"

I slammed the glass down in the sink and turned around. "Okay. So here's where that part about you owing me comes in."

"Huh?"

"I can't explain it all now. But I will. I promise. What I need from you, in the meantime, is to just go with it. Pretend like you know about the contest. Pretend that you're happy for me. But most of all, don't talk!"

"Wow." Sam took a step back and shook his head.

"What?"

"I hope you know what you're doing. 'Cause I sure as heck don't."

I picked up a triangle of toast and handed it to him. "It'll be fine. Come on." I walked to the hall and looked at myself in the mirror.

* * *

"Yoo-hoo! Has the fame already gone to your head?"

I looked at Kimmy. How long had she been talking to me? "I'm sorry, I was just thinking about Sam."

A chorus came from down the hall: "Congratulations, Sophie!" "Yeah, good luck!"

"Thanks," I said. I smiled and did a little beauty pageant wave.

"You did not just do the beauty pageant wave," Kimmy scoffed.

I stuffed my hand into my skirt pocket. "My bad," I said. Out of the corner of my eye, I saw a bunch of junior guys giving me the thumbs-up.

"What about Sam?" Kimmy asked.

"I'm obviously going to have to tell him everything. And then he'll kill me."

As if on cue, Michelle Alberghetti appeared before us. Even I could see why Sam was obsessed with her, with those big brown eyes and her thick sable mane. And the fact that she had to be a C-cup, and always wore tops that strained at the seams, didn't hurt.

"Sophie! You're the luckiest girl in the world!" she gushed.

I felt anger bubble up inside me, not just because she'd taken Sam's ring and played him for a fool, but because here she was envying me when she was the one who could have the real count if she just opened those heavy-lidded crème brûlée eyes of hers. "Hey. Thanks for returning Sam's ring the other night," I said, perhaps a little too sugary. "I heard you found it on the field."

"Oh, right, sure, no problem," Michelle said. Her cheeks caught fire.

"Yeah, funny, because he told me he'd put it in a chip bag and left it in his backpack but then you managed to find it on the field. I still can't understand *how*—"

"Sophie, come on," Kimmy said. She must've known what was coming.

"And then I started hearing these rumors about how you were *wearing* the ring at some dinner, and that the cheerleaders put you up to it—"

Kimmy pretended to look at her watch, only she wasn't wearing one. "Look at the time. We're going to be late!" She tugged at my elbow.

"But I can't believe you'd do such a thing, especially if you like my brother. Which you do, don't you? At least he thinks you do."

"Sophie!" Kimmy stomped her foot.

"I'm sorry, I gotta go," Michelle said. She put her head down and bolted through the doors to the math department.

"Was that an 'I'm sorry' for stealing my brother's ring? Or 'I'm sorry, I'm not listening to you anymore'?" I said to Kimmy. I took a deep breath.

"I suggest you chill out. Remember, you're the one who set this whole thing in motion. I wouldn't judge other people for getting swept up in the frenzy if I were you," Kimmy scolded. "I have English. I'll see you at our usual time, okay? Good luck." With that, she took off down the hall. I was on my own.

"Sophie!"

I turned. It was Destiny. She had evidently retired her count wear.

"Look, I just wanted to apologize for the way I treated you when you asked about my shirt. I never in a *million* years would have guessed *you* knew about—"

Yes, I get it. Unfathomable that I might be so cool. "Don't sweat it, Destiny," I said, then turned to walk away.

"Wait!" she called. I stopped. "I just . . . well . . . you know . . . if things don't work out between you and Count S, I was hoping maybe you could put in a good word for me." Destiny reached into her designer handbag and pulled out a card with her phone number and e-mail address printed on it. It was pink and had a unicorn in the corner. I looked up at her. What high school kid had business cards? Destiny looked hopeful. She began to chew on the ends of her hair. Someone must've told her once that hair chewing made her even more adorable.

I handed the card back to her. "Sorry," I said. "You had your chance and you blew it."

"What?"

Whoa. I had meant with Spencer, who in my mind had always been the real count. But there was no way anyone else knew that. Not even Kimmy. I felt sweat break out on my forehead. "I just meant with the contest. You know, you had your chance to write in and plead your case. I won fair and square. And by the way, who's to say things won't work out?"

Destiny rolled her eyes. "Let's get real," she said. "And another thing. Don't think Spencer dumped me for you. I saw what he wrote in your yearbook and it was all a big joke. We were *laughing* about it." I felt the breeze from her hair as she flew around and stormed off.

I stood there, stunned and speechless. What in God's name had Spencer written in my yearbook? I'd find out Sunday when Mom came home. My hands were shaking. *Please, God. Just let me get to my first class without another incident.*

No dice.

"Hey." It was Spencer. He was wearing a navy hoodie that made him look pretty darn incredible. He smiled, though his smile seemed darker than usual.

"Hey," I said. "Look, Spencer, I have to confess that I actually haven't gotten the chance to read what you wrote in my—"

"Lucky guy, that count," he cut in. Then he walked on down the hall.

I felt my heartbeat in my teeth. I guess at Putnam High, there were no secrets.

"And that's how I got into this mess," I said.

I had come home to an ambush. All day long, people had been asking Sam questions. Now he wanted answers.

Sam, who had had his head buried in his pillow the whole time I was telling him the story, finally came up for air. "Crap," he said. His face was crimson. "Did you pull it up?" He nodded at my laptop.

"Yup." I sat on the corner of his bed and handed him the computer. "Here it is."

Sam sat up and started reading.

"Start at the beginning, I guess," I said. I chewed on a fingernail.

As Sam scanned through all the blog entries and comments, one by one, my mind circled back on the day. I had to admit, being famous had had its initial thrill. It was fascinating to have my existence acknowledged by other human beings. People had been nice to me, complimenting me on how clever I must be to have landed such a prize. People were suddenly seeing me in a different light. There was more to Sophie Delorme, the former invisible kid. I was someone who'd achieved something grand. But how? Many kids, girls mostly, asked what I'd written in my entry, but I'd managed to avoid giving any direct answers. I think people believed what they wanted to believe, like the pervert Darrel Klein, who said I must have promised "the dude" "something dirty." Those who knew me better might have assumed I'd wowed him with my French. Kids under the popular misconception that I was a brainiac probably thought that I'd written something of literary merit.

Aside from my mind-numbing encounters with Destiny and Spencer, I'd had very few negative interactions. Even Michelle Alberghetti later singled me out in the halls and apologized for taking Sam's ring. She begged me not to tell him. I got the feeling she might actually like him after all.

"Who is this Celebstalker idiot?" Sam asked.

"'Idiot' is an understatement. He's the guy who sold the crest stuff. Read on." I wondered how many SOPHIE, HOW DO I HATE THEE? shirts he'd sold so far.

Sam looked up. "Who is this kid supposed to be? I mean this count. He doesn't sound a bit like me."

"I told you from the start, he was never you. He was just a figment of my imagination." More like Spencer. But there were some things that even my twin didn't need to know.

Spencer. I closed my eyes and saw him again, telling me the count was a lucky guy. How was I going to get my hands on that yearbook? I needed to get to Mom's car now, not Sunday. Maybe I could get Dad to drive me. Even then, how would I ever find it in the parking lot? And even if I did, I had no key. But maybe Dad did.

"When's Dad coming home?" I asked.

"Not till late," Sam said without looking up from the computer. "He has some alumni association dinner." Guess I'd just have to wait.

Finally, Sam closed the laptop. He couldn't be finished yet. "Damn, Sophie. I can see why this was so fun for you, the way this thing just caught fire. Everyone at school has been talking about it. But the family crest? I mean, did you really have to swipe the ring from my room in the middle of the night? You could have just ripped some design off the Internet. You made everything else up."

He was right. And I might have saved myself a lot of trouble if I had. "Sweat the details, I always say."

"I've never heard you say that."

I reached over and lifted open the computer screen. "Just keep reading."

A few more minutes went by. "It's funny, but I know you so well, I can hear your voice when I read these posts."

"Let's hope no one else can."

Sam looked up. "Who else knows?"

"Just Kimmy and Taylor."

"Taylor." Sam shook his head. "And she's actually the one who came up with the big scheme?"

"Can you believe it? I think we underestimated her."

"Yeah, we'll see." Sam shut the laptop again. This time he was apparently really done. "You think she'll stick around? I mean, after Dad talks to her and apologizes?"

I took the laptop from Sam. "Dad was going to talk to her today." I started to get up.

"She's not going to tell him about any of this?" Sam asked.

"What purpose would that serve? My only goal is to get this mess over with and move on with my old, insignificant life." I tucked the laptop under my arm.

"Think you'll be able to?" Sam scooted toward the end of the bed. "Maybe you'll become a fame junkie."

"Very funny." I didn't see any danger of that. As much as I enjoyed the initial attention (or lack of invisibility), I'd also seen what popularity could do to people. There are always people out there who are going to try to knock you down or, even worse, use you to get what they want—CELEBSTALKER19, then Destiny.

"It's going to be tough to pull this whole scheme off," Sam said.

"I know."

Then he caught me off guard. "What can I do to help?"

"You can't do anything, except maybe make sure Mom doesn't catch wind of what's going on. The last thing I need is her showing up at the big dinner." Just the thought of either parent showing up made me shiver.

"How am I going to do that?" Sam asked. He reached for some textbooks on his desk, then sat back down on the bed.

"Mom has no life other than working twelve hours a day. All you need to do is not open your mouth and accidentally blab to her about my date."

"Give me some credit, Soph." Sam yawned, making me realize he'd be out before he got into the first paragraph of whatever he had to read for school. Come to think of it, I was pretty tired myself. Fame had turned out to be exhausting. How did Beyoncé do it?

"I have to admit, it's a good plan. It could work," Sam added.

"We'll see." I had so much riding on Taylor's plan that I couldn't even bring myself to imagine all the things that could go wrong.

"Listen. Whatever you do tomorrow morning, don't ambush Dad with questions about Taylor. He'll talk when he's ready," I said.

"You got it," Sam said in a yawn.

Next morning, in the downstairs hall . . .

"So did you talk to Taylor? How did it go? Did you apologize? What did she say?" I had to stop to take a breath.

Sam shook his head. He was still on the stairs. "Really? This is your idea of not ambushing Dad?"

Dad laughed. I could already tell by his wide smile—the one we hadn't seen in weeks—that things must've gone well. "I called her and apologized for rushing to conclusions. She was understanding."

"That's great. So when are you going to see her to talk things out?" I asked.

"Really, Sophie." Dad shook his head and headed for the kitchen. Calvo appeared out of the shadows, hungry for kibble.

"Really *what*?" I asked.

The cat rubbed against Dad's leg. He batted him away, then turned around. "Some things can't be forced. You just need to let it happen."

"You've been *letting things happen* for three years," Sam chimed in, which surprised me a little. He rarely challenged Dad. And rarely got up before ten on a Saturday to begin with.

"You, too?" Dad smiled, shook his head, and went for the cat food in the cupboard.

"We just don't want to see you lose someone who's great and obviously important to you," I said in agreement with this impostor who'd replaced my brother.

Dad dumped a cupful of cat food into Calvo's bowl. The cat dove for it. "All right. If you must know, I asked her if she wanted to meet for dinner on Tuesday—"

Tuesday! That was the night of my big date! Taylor needed to be there!

Dad continued, "But Taylor said she had tutoring that night. And I have papers to grade all weekend. So we're meeting Monday night for a yoga class, and then we'll go somewhere for coffee afterward."

"*Yoga?*" Sam and I both said at the same time. I turned to my brother, who by now had made his way to the kitchen, and saw the expression of horror on his face, which I was sure was mirroring my own. Oh, the thought of our sweaty parent in downward dog or twisted up like some kind of pretzel in his gym shorts was simply too much to bear.

"I'm going to stick my head in the toilet and try to flush that image from my mind." Sam groaned. He shook his head as he made for the stairs.

"I'm not *that* inflexible!" Dad said, indignant.

"Sam, let me know if it works!" I hollered after my brother.

"Sophie, come on," Dad said. I headed for the stairs as well.

I could hear Dad's footsteps following me. "It's *yoga*! How hard can it be?"

"Right, Dad." I went to my room.

CHAPTER TEN

• •

Seeing as it was Saturday, Kimmy and I decided to stake out the restaurant where Count S and I would be having dinner. The Cheesecake Factory at the Putnam Mall wasn't exactly L'Espalier, but it would have to do. Somehow, the mall felt safe and familiar. And if you squinted, from the outside, the facade of the Cheesecake Factory looked a little like a château. Not really, but whatever.

"Should we make a reservation for Tuesday and ask for a dark, quiet corner somewhere?" I craned my neck to find a dark, quiet corner. The mall was jammed.

"I don't think they take reservations," Kimmy said. She took a sip of her iced tea. "And there are no dark, quiet corners. This is the Cheesecake Factory. But it'll be Tuesday night in the middle of a school week, so I doubt many people will be here."

"We hope," I replied. The waiter slid a plate holding an enormous wedge of sugary goodness onto the table.

"If you're worried people will come looking for you here, you can put something on the blog and on Facebook to throw them off the trail," Kimmy suggested.

"Great idea." I slid my fork into the sinful slice of white chocolate caramel macadamia nut heaven and all my problems vanished.

Kimmy pushed the plate toward me. "So, I have something I have to tell you. I thought about not telling you, because you have so much on your plate right now—"

"Ha! Literally," I said as I went in for another bite. "Sorry. Go ahead."

"But I decided to tell you anyway, because what kind of friend would I be if I didn't tell you something this life-changing and epic?"

Kimmy had a flair for hyperbole. I held up my fork and motioned for her to speed it up.

"So I was talking to Kelly Moses, who heard from Amy Van Horn, who found out from Destiny of all people that Spencer Kavanaugh likes you."

Had the cheesecake worked its way into my ear canals? I looked up. "What did you say?"

Kimmy smiled and folded her arms. "It's legit."

I reached for my water glass and washed down the cake. "You really think this is the time to goof on me?"

"No. Which is why I'm not. That's why I almost didn't even tell you."

"*Kimmy!*" I reached over and grabbed her by the sleeve of her hoodie. "What are you *saying*?"

She leaned back. "You know, if you think about it, there were signs. Like the tutoring—"

"So I'm a good French student."

"And the time we saw him in the parking lot with that cheerleader and he tried to pretend nothing was going on when he saw you walk by—"

"Oh, come on."

"And how he was nice to you after Destiny had been such a witch about the T-shirt. And maybe he really was looking your way and not at the clock that night at the soup kitchen. By the way, did you ever find out what he wrote in your yearbook?"

"No! It's still in Mom's car. But she comes home tomorrow."

"Did it ever occur to you that he might have switched books on purpose?"

Remarkably, it hadn't. And I hadn't yet told Kimmy about what he'd said yesterday about the count being a lucky guy. Oh my God, what if it was true? Still, I couldn't let myself believe it, especially after what Destiny had said.

"It could be Destiny just stirring things up," I cautioned. "Yesterday she was being all nice to me to try to get me to give her card to the count. When she realized she wasn't getting anywhere, she got nasty and said she'd read what Spencer had written in my book and that it was all a big joke."

"Must be something pretty nice, then." Kimmy reached over and scooped up some frosting onto her fork. "Amy Van Horn said she saw Destiny crying in the bathroom at the end of the day on Friday. I guess where Spencer's concerned, the joke's on her." Kimmy licked the icing off the fork.

I felt my face turning red and the warm rush of blood flowing out to my fingers. Could it really be true? The whole thing seemed terrifying, as "terrifying" seemed to have become my new world order.

"But why would he show her what he wrote to me?"

"Who says he did? How do you know she didn't just snoop?" Kimmy shrugged and leaned forward. "So? What do you think?"

"I have no idea what I think. I mean, it sounds crazy." Now that my stomach was flip-flopping, I sort of wished I hadn't eaten all that cheesecake.

"What are you going to do?" Kimmy asked.

"What *can* I do? I've got a date with a count in three days."

"Bet that whole thing made Spencer jealous."

"Oh, Kimmy."

She started to giggle. "We'd better go find you something to wear for your date on Tuesday. And maybe something for school on Monday while we're at it."

We flagged down the waiter, paid the check, and walked out to the entrance of the mall. Just as we stepped onto the concourse, two girls walked by in SOPHIE, HOW DO I HATE THEE? shirts. Kimmy elbowed me in the ribs.

"Did you see that?"

"Uh-huh." But I couldn't blame them. I had just learned that the hottest guy in my school had a thing for me. *Me*. Sophie *Nobody*. I'd managed to achieve both fame and infamy over the course of a few days, but none of that really mattered. All I could think about was that Spencer might actually like me.

> This Tuesday is the big night. Will Sophie Delorme find
> eternal bliss with Count Charming? Or will she be so
> nervous she spills soup on her shirt? (Sorry, Sophie. But
> as your competition, we must all hope for the worst.)

So the big question remains: where are they going to dinner? And how many of us are planning to crash the big date? We've been promised last-minute word of the secret location, but we haven't heard a peep from Count S or his posse about what he has planned. We're sure Sophie doesn't know, either. So let's hear some guesses from you.

We think he'll whisk her away to some fine French restaurant. But then again, he might try to throw off the masses and opt for some cozy pub or a Chinese restaurant. We've heard Count S does like his mai tais.

Adoringly, Mlle. Blogger

Within minutes comments started appearing.

I think he should have something catered in his hotel room. Then again, this Sophie chick is probably jailbait. High school? Really? WTFPEOPLE from Berlin, Germany

Hey, she won fair and square, which says something kind of pathetic about the rest of us. RINGMYBELLE from Charlotte, NC

Oh, SNAP. SECRETKEEPER from Glendale, AZ

He should rent out a whole restaurant so they can be alone. Yum. MARRYRICH from Santa Monica, CA

The most romantic thing for him to do is have dinner waiting
for her down on the Esplanade. Like a picnic.
BOSTONBABE

I make a mean mai tai.
GAYSIANJIM from New York, NY

Who ever heard of Putnam, Massachusetts? She could at least
have been from somewhere civilized.
QUEENBEE from Fire Island, NY

I bet Sophie wouldn't know foie gras if it bit her in the behind.
Such a waste.
BITTERSUE from Nantucket, MA

I let the debate rage on. Whenever anyone suggested that the dinner might take place in Putnam, I threw out a rumor about a shuttle to New York or a limo ride to the Berkshires.

Sunday afternoon, Dad dropped us off at Mom's, and I immediately set up camp in the condo parking lot.

"Aren't you coming upstairs?" Sam asked.

"Nope." I sat on the bench by the entrance to the building. "I'm waiting here for Mom."

"Whatever," he said, then disappeared through the door.

Moments later, Mom came through the gates. I ran to the car to greet her.

"Sophie, what a nice surprise!" She popped the trunk latch and got out of the car. "How was your week?"

"Great. Did you have a good trip?" There was the book, right where I'd left it on the backseat. I wrestled with the right rear door handle. "Can you unlock the door, Mom?" I heard the latch click open. "Can you believe it? I left my yearbook in the car." I opened the door and grabbed the book, then squeezed it to my chest.

"My, my, you couldn't wait to get your hands on that, could you?" Mom took her suitcase out of the trunk, then pulled at the handle so she could wheel it to the door. "Must be something juicy in there." We made small talk till we got to the condo. Her meeting had gone well. Nothing much going on at school, Dad was fine, you know, the usual. (*ARE YOU KIDDING?*)

Finally safe inside my room, with Mom unpacking and Sam watching a Red Sox game in the living room, I set the precious yearbook down on my desk and opened it. There was Kimmy's long entry on the inside front cover. I started flipping through the pages. My heart was thumping in my chest as I turned through the senior photos, then their baby pictures. (How I loved that new yearbook smell!) Next came the junior photos. I slowed down, looking for Spencer's handwriting, which I would easily recognize now, thanks to our tutoring session. I got to the *K*s, to Spencer's photo. Aside from his eyes being half shut, he looked dreamy. In fact, I thought the half-shut eyes were kind of movie-star bedroom-y. And there was a candid action shot of him playing lacrosse on the same page. But no signature. Well, where the heck did he sign it, then?

I flipped to the sports section, then the math team. I even flipped to my photo to see if he'd signed there. No, thank God. It was a horrible picture. My mouth looked like it had been pasted on crooked, and I had a rogue strand of hair sticking up from my part. I would have hated to think that I'd have to look at that picture every time I went to reread what Spencer had written to me, assuming it was something good, of course, and I really had no reason to expect that at all. And even if it was good, it could all be a joke, just as Destiny had said. My palms started to sweat. Maybe he hadn't signed it at all. Maybe *that* was the joke. Then, just as I was about to go back to the beginning once more, there it was, on the same page as a bad student-art rendering of the Putnam village green and the famous bronze sculpture of a little boy handing a girl a single rose bloom.

> Dear Sophie,
> I just want to tell you . . . I think you have the perfect . . . everything. I need to know you better.
> XO
> Spencer

By the fiftieth or sixtieth time through, I started to allow myself to believe that my eyes were not playing tricks on me, and that he had taken my suggestion for what to write in a girl's yearbook and written those very words to me, as though I had been the girl all along. Not yearbook cheerleader. Not Destiny. Me. Of course, as I'd been warned, this could still all be a joke. But for this moment I would allow myself to believe that what Spencer had written was how he truly felt.

If not for the forthcoming date with my imaginary count, I might have just keeled over and died at my desk. Happy.

*   *   *

It didn't take long for the magic to wear off. Regardless of what he'd written in my book, Spencer was clearly not happy with me now. And if the stress of facing him on Monday weren't enough, there was the Dad and Taylor drama to consider, and the upcoming date just two days away. This would not be a restful night. But before I even tried to shut my eyes, I needed to call Kimmy and tell her what Spencer had written. And then I wanted to talk to Taylor, just so she could reassure me with her calm demeanor that everything would be all right.

"Sophie? It's almost midnight." It sounded like I'd woken her up.

"I'm sorry, Taylor. I just wanted to make sure everything was all set for Tuesday," I said.

"Stop worrying. Everything will be fine."

That was what I needed to hear. "Okay. I'm sorry I woke you up." I hesitated. "Go easy on Dad tomorrow, okay?"

"Sophie, when have I ever been hard on your father?" she asked.

"I just mean with the yoga stuff. You break him, you buy him, okay?"

Taylor laughed. "I won't break him. And I know what you really mean. Don't worry. I'm open to whatever happens. We just have to allow things to unfold."

"I think Dad is a closet Buddhist." I yawned.

"Why's that?"

"Because that part about allowing things to unfold is more or less what he said, too."

"Go to bed, Sophie. And stop worrying. Things will be okay. You'll see."

"Thanks, Taylor. Good night."

"Good night," she said, then hung up.

By now you might have the mistaken impression that I'm closer to Taylor than I am to my own mother. That's not at all the case. It was just that I had been focusing so much on Dad and his relationship troubles, and had only just come to realize that Taylor is a pretty cool person. But despite Mom's working way too hard at the ad agency, we've always been close. Now it seemed her "mom-dar" was up.

When I arrived at breakfast, she was leaning over the kitchen island, reading the paper in jeans and a sweatshirt, rather than her usual bathrobe or office attire. It felt good to see her that way, no makeup, her blonde hair unwashed and up in an elastic band. I always thought she looked younger like that, without all the foundation, blush, and mascara she wore to make herself look younger.

"Are you feeling okay? You're not sick or anything?" I asked.

"I'm fine. Just going in a little later this morning," Mom answered. "Jet lag." She winked, came up and gave me a kiss on the cheek, held my face in her hands for a moment, then brushed the hair from my forehead. She stepped back and scanned my outfit. "When did you get that top? It's very sophisticated. I like it."

I was wearing my skinny jeans with a new black peasant blouse. "Kimmy and I went to the mall over the weekend."

"You and I are overdue for a shopping trip. I've been meaning to buy you a few things for summer, some shorts and tanks . . ."

"Sounds great."

Sam emerged from his room and took his seat at the table. Mom had cereal and juice poured for us. The comics section of the paper had been placed near his bowl.

"Morning, Samuel," Mom said. She tousled his hair and he grimaced, their daily ritual. She turned to me. "So, I get off work a little early tomorrow. What do you say we go then?"

"Go where?" Sam asked. He splashed milk from the pitcher into his cereal bowl.

"I want to take Sophie shopping," she said. She turned to the sink and poured water into the coffeepot. "We just have some catching up to do. You know, girl stuff."

My face must've betrayed my horror to my twin. I slid into the chair beside Sam.

"I need new cleats," Sam announced. "For the game on Wednesday. Mine are tight." He winked at me.

Mom sighed and turned back around. "A little more notice would be nice, Sam," she said. "We could go after supper tonight."

"Can't." Sam buried his face in the comics. "I have Frisbee and then there's a meeting for Montreal."

"Why don't you take Sam tomorrow?" I offered. I poured milk on my cereal. "I'd love to go shopping with you, Mom, but Kimmy has this science project, and I promised I'd help her."

"But it's not often I can get away in the late afternoon. I just thought you and I—"

"I really need to help Kimmy. She's freaked. Besides, I have plenty of stuff for school." I ate a spoonful of Cheerios. Unlike Dad, Mom never bought generic. "We could always go this weekend if you want."

"I suppose," Mom said. She sighed.

Crisis averted. Bullet dodged. And I had Sam to thank.

* * *

The instant I got off the bus, a group of freshman girls fell in step alongside me. At first, I thought they had me mistaken for someone else. This must be what fame was like to the newly famous. People start noticing you all of a sudden and you space and forget that you're famous. You look around and wonder who they're gawking at, and then you realize it's you. It's a little creepy.

As I made my way to the school entrance, more kids joined us, and by the time I reached the lobby, I had a full-blown entourage. So much for my worrying about being left alone with Spencer. Over the next two days, this "most popular kid in school" thing would probably continue. I figured if Spencer really liked me, he'd stick around until after Wednesday. Besides, I couldn't imagine anything like this happening to me again in my lifetime. I decided to run with it.

"Oh my God, you must be so excited," one of the freshmen said. The others shrieked.

"I am, I guess." I walked down the hall and stopped at my locker. The pack followed.

"What are you going to wear tomorrow night?" asked Kitty Davis, one of the school's biggest gossips.

"And where are you going? No one seems to know," chimed in Kelly Moses, who was gnawing on a pretzel stick.

"I have no idea. I'm not supposed to find out until right before." I entered my combination and opened my locker.

"How are you getting picked up? A limo?" another freshman asked.

"Has to be a limo," said another.

"He could be picking her up in his Lamborghini," suggested Amy Van Horn. "He has one, remember?"

Kitty rolled her eyes. "That has to be back in Europe. Duh." I had to hand it to these girls; they'd done their homework.

"Yeah, I don't know about any of that, either." I took two books out of my backpack, dumped them on the floor of my locker, and slammed it shut.

"I hear he is absolutely gorgeous!" Amy said.

"Sophie, what if he's really into you? Can you imagine the kind of life you'd lead?" Kelly asked. She hugged her binder.

"I doubt it'll go beyond one date," I said. "I'm still in high school."

"You better make sure you get a kiss from him at the end of the night," the first freshman said.

I felt my face heat up.

"He must be an amazing kisser," the second freshman said.

"Krista! What would you know about it?" the first one sniped.

The girls laughed.

Somehow, this human cluster had meandered down the hall without my even noticing. When I finally looked up, I realized we had parked ourselves in front of the boys' locker room. Standing two feet away, right in the doorway, was Spencer. His hair was wet, and he had his gym bag slung over his shoulder. He must've heard everything.

"Hi, Spencer," one of the girls said in a creamy voice.

"Hey," he replied. We made eye contact. He had a look on his face that I'd never seen before—disgust. He dodged the group and walked off.

For the rest of the day, I was invisible only where Spencer was concerned. Kimmy and I had been standing out in front of French class when he walked right by us and into the classroom without even looking up.

"So much for him liking me," I said. I felt sad, but also a little relieved that the old world order had been restored.

"He's just tweaked about your date," Kimmy reassured me. She stuck a wad of gum in her mouth.

I held out my hand, and she deposited a wrapped piece of gum into my open palm. I couldn't speak French with gum in my mouth, so I slipped it into my pocket for later. "Get real."

"He's jealous. He pours his heart out to you in your yearbook, which you never genuinely respond to or appear to even take the time to read, and next you're off on a date with someone who seemingly has a lot more to offer."

"If only that *someone* existed." Oh, the irony.

"Shhhh." Kimmy glared at me. She looked around to make sure no one had heard. "Spencer doesn't know any better."

"You know what would really suck?" I lowered my voice. "If this whole thing I made up ends up costing me a chance with him." Since it had been about him in the first place.

"You've just got to play it cool. Be excited about the date, but not too excited. And after the date, don't embellish," she said.

"Embellish *what?*"

"Lord knows. Look what you've managed to pull out of that brain of yours so far."

Fair enough. My backpack was getting heavy. I shifted it to the other arm. "We really haven't discussed any sort of post-date strategy."

"Debriefing. You're right." Kimmy tapped her finger against her lower lip. "We should just wait and see how things play out, and then we'll spin our story from there."

"Honestly, who *are* you? I think you've found your calling. You should be a publicist, or a politician, or something."

The bell finally rang.

"Yeah, I've been thinking about that. I'm good at this." Kimmy smiled. "I'll see you in study hall."

I entered the room where Spencer and I would sit for the next forty uncomfortable minutes.

To top off the day, as Kimmy and I were leaving the campus, we spotted Destiny and two of her friends wearing SOPHIE, HOW DO I HATE THEE? T-shirts.

I wondered what CELEBSTALKER19 would do after the date was over, and what I'd do with the blog, for that matter. But I had to focus on getting through the next day and a half. The rest would have to wait.

CHAPTER ELEVEN

• •

The big day has arrived. Plans are still being held close to the count's (manly) chest. All we know is that at some point during the next twelve hours, Sophie Delorme will be picked up at an undisclosed location to have dinner with Count S at another undisclosed location. Security appears to be tight as a result of all the Sophie-haters who have expressed their disdain in the form of a T-shirt. (We won't dignify the proprietor of said shirt by mentioning his name.) Isn't there enough of Count S to go around? Can't we all just get along?

Perhaps Sophie will be able to tell us more later. At the very least, we should finally have some photos of our beloved count posted right here by this time tomorrow. If anything breaks between now and this evening, you'll be sure to hear it here first. We have informants on high Count S alert strategically placed all over town and at the airport. And if any of you have any inside scoop, by all means let us know.

Good luck, Sophie! There are a lot of American women counting on you to represent us well. We're sure that's a lot of pressure riding on those young shoulders of yours.

Adoringly, Mlle. Blogger

"The best laid schemes of mice and men . . ." And to think we were actually reading this poem by Robert Burns in English class earlier today. How could I not take it as an omen? On the social front, Tuesday in school had gone down pretty much as Monday had, with kids following me around all day, attending to my every word and worshiping whatever secret wisdom they believed I held, whatever voodoo powers I might possess that had landed me this date. Spencer-wise, it had been the same as Monday. He'd gone out of his way to avoid me. That was until the final dismissal bell rang and he ambushed me in front of my locker.

"Hey, guys," Spencer said to my posse. He dropped his backpack and his workout bag at my feet. "Mind if I talk to Sophie alone for a minute?"

The group of mostly freshmen looked confused and/or annoyed but they scattered just the same.

"Hey," Spencer said to me after they were gone.

"Hey," I replied. My heart started beating so hard I felt like everyone in the whole school could hear it. I shut my locker.

"Ready for your big date tonight?" he asked.

The air rushed from my lungs. My back flattened against the lockers. "Before you say anything—" I started.

"Look, I can't blame you for wanting to go out with this guy.

From the looks of it, every girl in school wishes she were you."

I wanted to explain. I shook my head. "It's not like that—"

"What kills me is that I pretty much laid my heart on the line with what I wrote in your yearbook and you didn't even take the time to read it." Spencer lowered his head. I could tell he was genuinely hurt.

"I didn't read it because I accidently left the book in the backseat of my mother's—"

"So then you *lied* about having read it."

"Which I admitted I shouldn't have done. But I never expected you'd write something like that. I had no reason to," I said.

He raised his eyebrows. "Seriously?"

It suddenly struck me that Spencer was not used to being on this end of things. He was used to having every girl he so much as looked at fall to pieces. "Spencer, we barely *know* each other. And if you recall, right after our tutoring session that day, Kimmy and I saw you in the parking lot pinned to your car by that cheerleader."

He shook his head. "I knew that looked bad. I was trying to tell her I wasn't interested—"

"And then there you were in the hall with Destiny again a few days later."

"She came up to me. I had already told her I wanted to cool things off," he said.

"And speaking of Destiny, she told me what you'd written in my book was some big joke between you and her." There, I'd said it.

"What? How could she know what I'd written? When could she have . . . ?" He seemed adequately perplexed. Okay, so Destiny had spied without his knowing.

"I don't know, Spencer," I said. I folded my arms and stared at him. It appeared we had reached a stalemate. What were we even arguing about? Just then, I spotted Kimmy by the stairwell. She was waving for me to come over. Was she out of her mind?

Spencer ran his hand through his hair. "Look, this is crazy. The truth is I meant what I wrote in your yearbook. They were your words, but they said exactly how I felt. I like you, Sophie. I have for a while." He dropped his gaze.

Warm honey in the veins, that's the only way I can explain how I was feeling. "How come?" I pressed. Even I couldn't see how it was possible. I needed to know.

Spencer took a step back and laughed. *"How come?"* he repeated. "Because you're smart and funny . . . and beautiful."

I felt my face heat up.

"And you seem to care about the right stuff, you know, helping people out. I was really surprised you were wrapped up in all this count stuff, which Destiny had obviously filled me in on. And then when I heard you actually won the contest, I didn't know what to think." He brushed the hair out of his eyes with his fingertips.

"I entered just for the heck of it. I never thought I'd win. Not in a million years."

Spencer leaned closer, resting his palm on the locker above my head. "So then if you don't really care about this guy, don't go. Let someone else go on the date. I'll take you to dinner somewhere tonight, just the two of us." His face was inches from mine.

Every organ, every bone, every molecule in my body wanted to say "Yes! Let's forget about Count S and go to dinner. Just the two of us." And yet I couldn't. Too many people had gone to too much trouble to help me out. This thing I had created was now bigger than I was. I had to go. My reputation—my family name, even—was at stake.

By now, Kimmy was waving both arms like a crossing guard. Whatever it was, it had to be important.

"I can't back out now, Spencer. I really wish I could. But I just can't." I didn't dare look at him as I said it.

Spencer let his arm drop. He rubbed his neck. "Suit yourself," he said. He shook his head, bent down to pick up his backpack and his workout bag, and headed off down the hall.

I wanted to cry. If it weren't for Kimmy, practically doing gymnastics in the doorway to the staircase, I probably would have.

When I reached the stairs, I lashed out at her. "What! What is it? What's so darn important?"

"It's gone viral!"

"What?" What the heck was she talking about?

"Tonight, the date. I guess the whole story got picked up by Gawker.com, then it was retweeted by some big-time event planner in Los Angeles who has thousands of followers. Anyway, it doesn't matter how it happened. What matters is everyone from Perez Hilton to Paris, France, knows about your dinner tonight. The press is gearing up as we speak. There are going to be reporters from all over the country there tonight."

"But no one even knows where we're going," I said, still in shock.

"They'll catch on eventually. They'll find out where you live and follow us."

I imagined reporters and photographers camped out on Dad's lawn or in front of Mom's condo. Thank goodness Dad wouldn't be home till after work and Mom and Sam were going shopping. Still, what would Mom and Dad do when they found out? Because there was no way they were not going to find out. Not anymore. "So I can't go home. We'll have to go straight to the mall from here," I said.

"We can go to my house first. You can borrow something of mine to wear. We can't take the school bus. We'll have to get someone to drive us."

"Oh my God, Kimmy, this is scary!"

"And a little exciting," she said. Kimmy was clearly in her element. "And don't think you're going to get off not telling me what just happened. Let's go find Jimmy Tucker and that car of his. Start from the beginning."

"Sophie, may I present to you the esteemed Count S," Taylor said. She smiled and curtsied. "Count S, Sophie."

I reached out to shake his hand. He bowed, then took my fingers in his and pressed his lips to the back of my hand. I felt goose bumps. A camera flashed. It was Kimmy's. She had gone from publicist to official event photographer. No one else from the press had shown yet. Maybe they wouldn't.

"That was *awesome*," Kimmy said. "He's *good*. Way to go, Taylor."

"What does the *S* stand for?" he asked.

"Apparently, *sexy*," Kimmy said.

I glared at her, then looked back at Taylor's cousin, Kardos. "It really doesn't stand for anything." I realized he was still holding my hand. Embarrassed, I slipped it out of his warm grip. "Thank you so much for doing this, Kardos," I added.

LYNN KIELE BONASIA

"My pleasure," Kardos said. His accent wasn't French, but to the untrained ear it was sufficiently foreign and dreamy.

"Why don't you guys go on over to your table?" Taylor said. She had her hair pulled back in a ponytail and was wearing a FREE TIBET baseball cap. "Kimmy can take some paparazzi shots behind the potted plants and then we'll just hang out here at the bar and keep watch."

"Do you think anyone will show?" I asked.

"It's a good sign if they haven't yet," Kimmy said, in truth sounding a bit crestfallen.

"Should we order something?" I asked.

"Maybe some dessert, for the pictures, so it looks like you were here for a while," Taylor suggested.

The hostess appeared behind Kimmy. "Excuse me, folks. You're going to have to clear the aisle so the servers can get through." She had chemically amped red hair and was wearing earrings with black spike balls. There couldn't have been more than ten people in the restaurant, but I wasn't about to argue with her. At least Kimmy had been right. It looked like it would be a slow night at the Cheesecake Factory.

"Shall we?" Kardos stuck out his elbow for me to slip my arm into. From behind, I saw another camera flash.

As Kardos and I took our seats at a table for two at the far end of the restaurant, I had my first chance to take a real look at him. Before this, I'd only seen him that once in front of Starbucks with Taylor. He'd been wearing a hat and facing away from us, but I had taken note of his physique, as I'm sure Dad had, too. He was a good-looking guy, sideburns and all. Tall but not too tall. Fit and lean. There was a grace to his movements. He was very debonair. Now, from the front, I could see how handsome he was. Perfect Count S material if I did say so myself, though not a bit like Spencer. Kardos had almost black hair that he wore in a purposefully mussed style. His eyebrows were thick and dark and framed his eyes, which were precisely the color of toasted almonds, just as I had said in the blog. He had a Roman nose, which was a little off from my Count S description and might have been too big for his face if his other features hadn't pulled their weight. Obviously, he didn't resemble my count to a tee, but I had never been too detailed about his likeness in the first place, always leaving some room for interpretation, thank goodness.

I eased into the seat. He pushed it in from behind. At least I felt pretty in the new borrowed dress Kimmy and I had picked out for her the other day, a blue three-quarter-sleeve mini with a delicate black swirl pattern woven into the fabric. Kimmy had helped me straighten my hair, and we'd sneaked into her mom's jewelry box and borrowed a few simple long gold chains. "You have no idea how much you're saving my life," I said to Kardos.

He sat. "Taylor gave me some idea." His eyes were captivating, and when he smiled, porcelain flashed so bright I thought Kimmy had taken another snapshot.

I took the napkin off my plate, shook it out, and draped it over my lap, painfully aware of my table manners, as if I might actually be dining with a nobleman. "So you hadn't seen each other for five years?" I asked. "Did you used to be close?"

"Our fathers are brothers. My family would come to the U.S. once or twice a year, and the whole family would get together,"

Kardos explained. He used his hands a lot when he talked. I thought he might take out a water glass. "Taylor was the oldest, and used to babysit us when our parents went out. My brothers and I all had a crush on her." He leaned in and reached for his napkin. "Completely innocent, of course. She is almost fifteen years older than I am."

"I bet she was pretty then," I said.

"And still."

"Oh, I know, I didn't mean . . ." If Sam were here, he'd be saying "Good one, Soph."

"I know. Some women have the good fortune to stay beautiful all their lives." Kardos winked. He reached out, grabbed my hand, and gave it a squeeze. For a moment I thought he was hitting on me. I felt my heart speed up. Then the camera flash brought me back to reality. Another photo op.

If I didn't think too hard about how contrived this all was, I could almost imagine that I was on a date with a real, live count. After all, this was a perfect stranger. He was handsome and sophisticated. I felt butterflies trying to kickbox their way out of my stomach. Wouldn't it be too much to take, my developing a crush on this figment of my imagination or, worse, my father's girlfriend's cousin? That's right: note I said *girlfriend* and not *ex-girlfriend*. Last night, I'd called Dad after his yoga adventure, and he'd told me things had gone well. (Though it was eleven P.M. and he was still icing his lower back.) He and Taylor had gone to a teahouse after class and talked for a couple of hours. Dad had apologized for everything, most of all for making her feel like she didn't matter to him. And they both agreed to give it another shot. After that, Dad invited me to go for our rain-checked ice cream tonight, but I told him that Kimmy and I had stuff to do, which at least wasn't a total lie, like the one I'd told Mom. I had felt bad about that. I didn't like lying to my parents.

The waitress came up to the table. "Can I get you something to drink?" She ogled Kardos, as I expected any woman with a pulse might.

"Sophie?" Kardos asked.

"Coke, please," I said.

"Do you have any French cab by the glass?" he asked.

"We do," she said.

"Um, Kardos? You're too young to order wine." I winked at him.

"You are?" the waitress said.

"I am?" He laughed. "Of course I am. I'll have a Coke. And just some dessert menus please. *Merci*." She left.

"Sorry about that," I said. I felt a smile on my face, quite possibly the first all night. "You're good. How do you say 'thank you' in Hungarian?"

"Köszönöm szépen."

"Yeah, I'll stick to French." We both laughed.

"Can you see anything going on up there? Have any people shown up?" I asked. I didn't want to turn around, but I sensed more people in the room.

Kardos sat tall and scanned the mall entrance. His brow furrowed a bit. "Just Taylor and your friend," he replied. "And the people who were here when we got here."

"Phew." I relaxed into my chair.

Kardos tapped my hand with his palm. "We'll get through this," he said encouragingly. He looked around the restaurant. "No one would suspect this place. Trust me."

"Not exactly big with the Euro set, I imagine."

Kardos laughed. More camera flashes. I wished Kimmy would knock it off. She was way overdoing it.

The waitress brought our sodas and handed us the dessert menus. It occurred to me that I was sitting at a table in a restaurant with a man who was not my father, yet who was old enough to be ordering drinks, had I allowed him to. It felt a little dangerous. I picked up my Coke and pretended it was an espresso martini.

"To new friends," Kardos said. We clinked glasses. Another flash.

"You're going to have to clear the aisle and stop doing that," I overheard the hostess tell Kimmy. The woman's shrill voice had to be more disruptive to the people eating there than Kimmy's picture taking.

"Sure, no problem," a male voice said. A bar stool screeched against the wood floor.

"Who are you people, anyway?" the hostess asked. "The press is not allowed in here. This is a private restaurant. You need to step back to the entrance or I'll call the cops."

I turned around. The second I did, I was blinded by what seemed like twenty flashbulbs going off at once. A big group of paparazzi were poised in front of the bar.

"Kardos! Why didn't you tell me they were here?"

"Just ignore them. They're moving back to the mall entrance. They're not allowed to be in here. They know the rules." He sipped his Coke. "So, does a pretty girl like you have a boyfriend?" he asked. He was trying to get me to relax. Wrong subject.

I took a deep breath. "Not likely," I said.

"What do you mean?"

"There's a boy I like at school, and he supposedly likes me, but he asked me not to go out with you tonight and there was obviously no way I could do that, given the circumstances."

"I see," Kardos said. He frowned.

"Anyway, there was an unpleasant exchange and I think I hurt his feelings." I felt a little pressure at the corners of my eyes. To forestall the waterworks, I picked up my fork and began inspecting it.

Kardos shook his head. "You underestimate yourself."

I set the fork down. "Huh?"

"You're a beautiful woman. Men are going to flock to you. Get used to it." Kardos took a sip of his Coke. I saw another camera flash and heard more feet shuffling behind us.

"It's all cool, Soph," Kimmy called to me.

I nodded but didn't dare turn around.

"You two are good friends," Kardos said.

"The best, actually."

The waitress appeared. We agreed to split a slice of cheesecake rather than each getting our own. More intimate. Plus, I knew how huge the slices were. Kardos asked if we might try the Chocolate Oreo Mudslide because it sounded so American.

"*Un Oreo Mudslide au Chocolat, s'il vous plait,*" Kardos said to the waitress. She looked at him like he was from Mars. She left.

"Do you speak French?" I asked.

"A little. Taylor told me about your family legacy. Pretty impressive."

"For my *brother*, anyway."

"*And* for you. The title isn't everything. Your family is part of

French history. You should find out more about it. Learn all you can. I'm sure you'll discover lots of things to write about." He winked.

Moments later, the waitress came back with the cake, a new hairdo, and fresh lipstick. I suddenly realized how hungry I was, and dove in. Kardos followed suit.

"Heaven," he said.

I nodded. "So you head back to Hungary tomorrow?"

"Great timing, yeh?" He grinned.

I was about to respond when I heard even more commotion at the front of the restaurant. I froze. I should have known things had been going too well. I strained to hear what was happening, but they had turned up the music. "Kardos . . ."

He was watching the entrance, too. "A man is pushing through the photographers to where Taylor and your friend are. Now he's talking to Taylor."

"A man? What does he look like?"

"American. Tall, a little gray at the temples. He's wearing baggy pants and a plaid shirt, and a sweater with patches at the elbows and—"

"Oh my God. Dad!" I jumped from my seat. Sure enough, there he was beside Taylor. His face was red. I ran to them. Flashbulbs blinded me. I reached out.

Dad saw me and grabbed my hands and pulled me close. "Sophie! There you are! What are you doing here? What's going on? Who's *that?*"

I turned and saw Kardos behind me. Kimmy snapped a photo.

"Kimmy, knock it off!" I said through my teeth.

"My bad," she said, hiding the camera behind her back.

"That's my cousin, Kardos," Taylor said. As he approached, Taylor made the introduction. "Kardos, this is Hal. Sophie's father."

Kardos nodded.

Dad had a corn kernel on his sweater. "I don't understand. I was home eating my dinner when the doorbell rang. I opened the door and there had to be twenty photographers on the lawn. *Why? What happened?* I started to panic. Had something happened to the kids? 'Where's Sophie?' they wanted to know. 'Who are you? Why are you here?' I asked. 'Is she okay?' "They told me you had won some kind of contest where the prize is dinner with a count. I thought it was some misunderstanding to do with the family title. Anyway, they said you might be headed to the airport or to a hotel in Boston with some kid who was almost twenty." Dad stopped to wipe the sweat from his upper lip. "They quickly realized I had no idea what they were talking about. I went inside and tried to call your mother and got no answer. Then I remembered you said you were with Kimmy, so I called her house."

"Uh-oh," Kimmy said.

Dad continued, "Her mom said you'd both gone to dinner at the Cheesecake Factory in the mall. . . ."

My jaw dropped. I looked at Kimmy. She shrugged. "Who were they going to tell?" she said. "They're even more clueless than your parents." As soon as she realized what she'd said, she winced.

Dad shot her a look. He went on, "I grabbed my keys and got into my car. But those photographer clowns were still out there and no sooner did I pull out of the driveway than they started to follow me." I couldn't think of the last time I'd seen Dad this agitated. I felt terrible.

Taylor got up. She had already flagged the bartender for a glass of water and handed it to Dad. "Why don't you sit here for a minute?" she suggested. She picked the corn off his sweater.

"I'm fine," he insisted. "Suddenly, here I was on this high-speed chase around Putnam." (A high-speed chase in a Prius?) "I finally lost them, or thought I did, and I walked in here, and here *you* are"—he pointed to Taylor—"and *you*"—he pointed to me—"and *you*"—he pointed to Kardos. Dad's brow got heavier. I thought he might try to punch Kardos. He turned to Taylor. "Why in the world would you be setting up my daughter with some nineteen-year-old playboy—"

"Twenty-three, actually," Kardos said.

"You're not helping," Taylor said to her cousin. "I told you, Kardos is my cousin. And I wasn't setting him up with Sophie, for God's sake, Hal. I was just trying to help her out of this mess."

"What *mess?*" Dad said, a little too loud.

I saw the hostess on her way over. I shook my head at her. "Dad, calm down. We're in a restaurant, okay?" I urged. The hostess backed off. She'd clearly given up on the prospect of any paying customers and was just focused on the restaurant's not being trashed on her watch.

"What . . . *mess?*" Dad repeated. Frustrated, he turned toward the mall entrance at the precise, unfortunate moment that Sam was pushing through the photographers, with my mother and her shopping bags trailing behind.

"Sam! Come back here!" Then she saw us. "Sophie?"

"Sam? Ellen!" Dad shouted. Another flurry of flashbulbs.

I had wondered if this could get any worse. I got my answer. What were they doing here? I wanted to strangle Sam.

"Whoops," Sam said. He looked like he wanted to crawl under a table.

"Hal?" Mom was surprised. "Sophie! What are you doing here?" She was still dressed for work and had obviously picked Sam up and come straight here. So even if there were photographers staking out the condo, she wouldn't have seen them.

I opened my mouth to answer but didn't get the chance.

I glared at Sam. "I'm sorry! I saw the photographers and thought there was something cool going on here, like maybe Tom Brady and Gisele were having dinner."

"At the *Cheesecake Factory?*" Kimmy and I said in unison. I was steaming. Never mind. They were here now. I had to deal.

"Sophie! You told me you were helping Kimmy with a project," Mom said. Her voice had begun its climb in pitch. "Why are these camera people here?"

"It is a project, sort of," Kimmy jumped in. Mom saw her for the first time. Kimmy raised her hand in a lame wave. "Hi, Ms. Ackerman."

Meanwhile, I glared at Sam.

"Don't look at me! How was I supposed to know which mall you were going to? I thought you meant the Arsenal. You know I get my cleats here at the Glentree."

Why would I know that, oh self-absorbed brother?

"What the heck is going on?" Mom finally raised her voice above all the others. More flashbulbs went off.

"I wish I knew," Dad said.

"And who's *that*?" Mom pointed at Kardos.

"That's Taylor's cousin," Dad said. At that moment, Dad must've realized he'd uttered his girlfriend's name in front of his ex-wife for the first time. He fell silent for a moment, then mustered the courage to move ahead. "Ellen, this is Taylor. Taylor . . ."

Taylor stuck out her hand. "Pleased to meet you, Ellen."

Mom shook. "Likewise, Taylor." More flashes. Did these guys even care what they were capturing?

Perhaps empowered by the renewal of his commitment to Taylor the night before, Dad continued. "You should know I've been seeing Taylor for a while now, Ellen," Dad said. "As in *dating*," he added.

The two women looked at each other and grinned. Mom shrugged. Taylor shook her head.

"What's funny?" Dad looked bewildered.

"Never mind, Hal," Taylor said. "Sophie, it's time you explain."

I motioned for my parents to come closer. No need for the press to hear this. Then I started from the beginning. I told them how on the day I'd found out I wouldn't inherit the title of countess, I'd felt cheated. So Taylor had suggested I write about my feelings. "Did you know Taylor is a writer, Dad?" I interrupted myself.

"*I* did," Mom said. She winked at Taylor.

Dad looked at Mom and raised his eyebrows. He shook his head and looked at Taylor. "I do now. I mean, I only just very recently found out," he said.

Before I continued, I looked toward the door. Fortunately, the militant hostess was keeping the photographers at bay at the entrance. "So, I know this wasn't what Taylor had in mind when she made the suggestion, but I started this blog where I made up adventures about a mysterious count who'd just landed in the States. Just to imagine what that kind of life might be like, only I wanted to do it from a guy's point of view rather than a girl's, because I didn't want anyone to know it was me, not that they would have, I guess. But I was sort of paranoid. I also thought girls would be the ones reading something like this, and that I'd attract more readers if I was writing about some awesome guy." Without thinking, I looked over at Kardos. He smiled. I felt my face heat up a little. What I didn't tell them was that writing about a male count allowed me to act out my fantasies of Spencer. "The next thing I knew, the whole thing had gotten way out of hand. People started looking for proof that the count existed. I panicked and posted a photo of the signet ring."

"You *what?*" Dad said. He took a gulp of Taylor's water.

"That was bad, I know. And then someone took the crest and made T-shirts out of it, and people were wearing them at school," I said.

"They *what?*" Dad said.

"Try to keep up, Dad." Sam shook his head.

I went on, "Then, later, people wanted to see pictures of the count. Of course, there *was* no count, so to distract them I came up with this contest where someone would win a night on the town with Count S."

"As in Samuel?" Mom asked. "I'm sorry. I'm confused."

"I just used that letter. Count S like 'countess.' Get it? As in what I am not?" Apparently, I still was having trouble letting that one go. "Anyway, I'll admit I didn't really think the contest thing through. Kimmy was the one who made me realize the only way out of all this was to make myself the winner. I needed to take control and stage the whole thing. And Taylor was kind enough to lend us her cousin here, who happens to be headed back to Hungary tomorrow."

"So how many people do you think actually saw this blog of yours?" Dad asked.

"I don't know. You see the people here. At this point, probably thousands. I've had comments from people in France and Germany and New York and Iowa and all over Massachusetts and—"

"You have to admit, that's pretty impressive," Kimmy said.

Mom and Dad just looked at her.

"But what are the odds that people here in this town would see it?" Dad asked. "It doesn't make sense. It's just too coincidental."

He was right. I really hadn't thought of it like that. Chalk this one up to *my* being self-absorbed.

"I suppose some of that could be my fault," Kimmy said. She stepped forward.

"Huh?"

"I sort of posted a link on Facebook, where everyone at school saw it and posted it to their pages," Kimmy explained. She turned to me. "I told you I knew about Count S. I even sent you a link before you told me about it all. You mustn't have opened it." I shook my head. *Obviously*. "The only part I didn't tell you was that I actually had already sent it out to my high school friends on Facebook. That included you, but you obviously haven't been paying attention to my posts." Who had time to pay attention to Facebook with all that had been going on?

"But how did you find out about it?" Mom asked Kimmy.

Kimmy looked at me and cringed a little. "I follow celebstalker. com," she answered. That part didn't surprise me at all. Like I said, she was always up on the latest sites and viral crazes. "That site is huge right now. Kids in California buy all his stuff. Then you see celebrities wearing it in *InStyle* and *People*, and on TV—"

"You mean that creep who cashed in on our crest with those T-shirts?" Sam asked.

"Our family crest? What gives him the right?" Dad's face was red.

It seemed Mom couldn't care less about the T-shirts. She turned to my brother. "And how long did *you* know about this?" she asked.

Sam shrugged.

"Kimmy, why didn't you tell me about the Facebook post sooner?" I asked.

"I felt horrible. I mean, here I am, your best friend, and chances are no one in town would have known about any of this if it wasn't for me." Kimmy fiddled with the camera strap. "I planned to tell you just as soon as I helped get you out of this."

I couldn't be mad at her. She didn't know I had anything to do with Count S.

Just then, a scream punctured my eardrums, followed by a frenzy of flashbulbs. We all turned to the mall entrance, and there were Destiny and a few other girls I recognized from school, push- ing their way through the ever-growing crowd of photographers. They must have been there on their nightly shopping excursion.

"It's *him*!" Destiny shrieked. "Look, there's Sophie! They're on their *date*!"

"Kardos, we have to get out of here." Taylor jumped off the bar stool and grabbed her cousin by the arm. "I don't want anything messing with your flight home tomorrow."

Lights blinded us and flashbulbs popped.

"I thought I'd lost them," Dad said. He put his wrist to his eyes to block the flashing. "They must've seen my car in the lot."

I had to let Dad believe that his high-speed chase resulted in the press coming here, even though the idea was ridiculous. Most had gotten here before he had.

"We'll go out the back. I'm parked close," Taylor said, calm as ever. "Call me later, Hal."

"Bye, Sophie. It was a pleasure. I wish you the best." Kardos reached down and took my hand. He kissed it the way he had before. This time, the photographers beat Kimmy to the flash.

I curtsied. The cameras caught that, too.

"Okay, knock that off," Dad said to Kardos and me. I looked over at Mom, who seemed also to be under Kardos's spell.

Destiny and her entourage tried to push their way past the hostess to the aisle leading to the back door, the one Taylor and Kardos had just slipped out. The hostess went charging after them. She grabbed Destiny's handbag and Destiny nearly fell backward.

"Hey!" Destiny screamed.

"Where do you think you're going? These restrooms are for customers only. Are you here for dinner?"

The girls gaped at her.

"We just want to go out the back!" Destiny said. She tried to slide past again, but the woman with the red hair and spike ball earrings threw herself in front of Destiny just in time. This hostess sure was over the top, but I was glad she was on our side now.

"I'm sorry, *that's* an emergency exit. You need to use the mall exit. We can't have people cutting through here. This is a *restaurant*. People are trying to enjoy their meals."

By this time, the dining room was empty. I did notice that Kardos had thrown some bills down on the table. A class act, through and through. "It's too late, he must be gone by now," one of the girls whined.

Destiny turned back toward the rest of us. She glared at me.

Sam took a step so that he stood between me and Destiny. "Get lost," he said.

Mom leaned closer to Dad. "Do you see what her shirt says? 'Sophie, how do I hate thee?'" Mom turned to me. She looked horrified. "Does she mean *you*?"

I nodded proudly. A little messed up, I know. But no matter how you looked at it, all of this had managed to come out of my own sweet and twisted brain.

"You girls, go on home," Dad said to Destiny and her friends.

They stomped off in their heels. It was only then that I realized that the photographers had already left. They must have scrambled to chase down the count. I hoped that Taylor and Kardos would make it out of the parking lot in time. Kardos was staying at some crappy hotel next to the airport because of his early flight the next morning. If Taylor could just get him there, they'd never find him.

"Let's go home," I said to Mom.

"What about your cleats, Sam?" she asked.

"I never really needed them," he said. This was one of those times when I loved my brother.

CHAPTER TWELVE

• •

Well, devoted followers, the bad news is, we never did get word of where Sophie and the count were until the date was all over. The good news is, this morning we have Sophie here with us for a live chat.

Mlle. Blogger: Sophie, you must be exhausted. Thanks so much for talking with us so early. Obviously, we're all dying to know: what was he like?

Sophie: I see you've posted some pictures here, so you know how good-looking he is.

Mlle. Blogger: Dreamy. Did his personality live up to his looks?

Sophie: He was charming. And very classy. He did things like kiss my hand and push my chair in for me. No one's ever treated me that way before.

Mlle. Blogger: Were you nervous?

Sophie: Totally. I think I was shaking at one point. But he was very nice. He put me at ease rather quickly.

Mlle. Blogger: What did you guys talk about?

Sophie: Lots of things. He told me about his family back home, how it looked like there was the slightest chance his parents might reconcile. He confessed how difficult the whole thing had been, and how, sometimes, all the fame and money in the world can't fix the things that really matter to us. He was surprisingly grounded.

Mlle. Blogger: That's refreshing. What else did you discuss?

Sophie: He told me about all the places he'd traveled to recently. Hungary, South Africa, Fiji, Marrakech . . .

Mlle. Blogger: We have to ask, you know, him being a jet-setter and all, why the Cheesecake Factory?

Sophie: LOL. That choice had absolutely nothing to do with him. It's embarrassing to say, but my parents insisted that the dinner be somewhere in Putnam. They were also really concerned that fans and reporters would crash the dinner, so they wanted to pick someplace that would be relatively quiet on a weeknight but offered some security in case things got out of hand. In the end, it worked out well for him, too.

Mlle. Blogger: . . . when fans and photographers actually did show up.

Sophie: He had someone with him keeping an eye out for trouble at the bar. When things got crazy, they were able to quickly make their escape out the back door.

Mlle. Blogger: In some of the pictures that have popped up on other sites, there's an older man and woman. Are they your parents?

Sophie: Yes.

Mlle. Blogger: Did they insist on going on the date with you?

Sophie: I'll admit, my parents are protective, but I am fifteen. What can I say?

Mlle. Blogger: Where did he want to take you before they laid down the law? Do you know?

Sophie: Ha! He wanted to take me to some cozy French restaurant in Vermont. He had a private plane on the tarmac at Logan in case my parents changed their minds.

Mlle. Blogger: *Très romantique!*

Sophie: Tell me about it.

Mlle. Blogger: Now, we'd like to open up the floor to our fans out there. You've been sending e-mails with questions, so if you don't mind, Sophie, maybe you could answer some of them.

Sophie: Certainly.

Mlle. Blogger: From FRANCAISKAY in Hoboken, New Jersey: What did he order?

Sophie: He had a Coke and a goat cheese salad. We split a slice of cheesecake.

Mlle. Blogger: From GOTHGIRL in North Conway, New Hampshire: Did he try to make a move on you?

Sophie: No, he was a perfect gentleman. He was very affectionate, holding my hand or putting his arm around me as we walked, but I think that's just a European thing.

Mlle. Blogger: From KEEPTHEFAITH in Harrisburg, Pennsylvania: Did he tell you where he was going next?

Sophie: Back to Europe. He was supposed to be leaving today.

Mlle. Blogger: From RINGMYBELLE in Charlotte, North Carolina: Sophie, why do you think he picked you?

Sophie: That's a good question. I'm really not sure. Once I met him, I could see we had a similar way of looking at things, despite his lavish lifestyle. My family is French, so that might have had something to do with it, but then again, he dates women of all nationalities. My guess is that he saw a highly public date with a fifteen-year-old high school kid as a way to stay out of trouble. LOL. I mean, with my parents right there, this wasn't going to turn into some new international scandal.

Mlle. Blogger: I suppose not. But did you feel any chemistry?

Sophie: Truthfully, beyond friendship, no.

Mlle. Blogger: What if he called you next week? Would you go out with him again?

Sophie: I don't think so. I mean, my entering this contest was really just curiosity. Like I said, I came from a French family and have probably always romanticized certain things about the French. But I don't have to look to France to find people I'm attracted to or care about.

Mlle. Blogger: Hmm, sounds like you have someone in mind?

Sophie: Okay, now I'm blushing. There's someone I like. But he wasn't thrilled about my going out on this date. So I'm not sure if he'll still be speaking to me when I get back to school. But I do like him, if he happens to be out there. And I'm sorry, for whatever it's worth.

Mlle. Blogger: Do you want to tell us his name?

Sophie: Seriously? I've become more famous than I can bear. Why would I do that to someone else?

I finished off the last question as the sun came up, and posted the interview (my three A.M. brainchild) just as I heard Mom moving around in her bedroom. I also uploaded photos from Kimmy's camera to my laptop last night before Mom came into my room and finally ordered me to bed, threatening to shut off the electricity. Even then, I couldn't sleep. I was so wired, relieved that the day was over and that things hadn't completely blown up in my face, trying to replay the whole night over and over in my mind. Sure, I'd have some penance to serve for Mom and Dad, like I'd probably be grounded for a while, but I didn't think they'd come down too hard on me. After all, the family legacy they'd recently sprung on us was at the root of all this. I'd never intended to hurt anyone (and still felt some remorse over that poor lady who had mortgaged her cat to buy count paraphernalia). I imagined, too, that I'd get a lecture from Dad about posting personal information on the Internet, which I deserved. How stupid do you have to be to put your name and the town you live in on a Web site? I made sure the photos I posted this morning were mostly all Kardos and just a little of me from the back. It was the other photographers who'd posted the rest. I found some of those shots already up on a few celebrity gossip sites when I searched "Count S." As for CELEBSTALKER19, I saw this morning that I was no longer hated, or at least he'd stopped selling the T-shirts. Late last night or early this morning, he had posted a small photo of Count S with the caption *The fabulous Count S on his date with a prom queen*. Sorry to disappoint, CELEBSTALKER19, but I am no prom queen. In any case, if the new feature splashed across the home page of his site was any indication (about a scandal involving a Spanish actress who was seen leaving an Italian night club half-naked and draped over the arm of a powerful German government official's son, who was gorgeous, I might add), Count S was already old news. This was further evidenced by the new bikini bra for sale, one side made from the flag of Spain, the other from the flag of Germany. I had to admit, the guy had a flair for opportunistic merchandising. I wondered whether our performance last night had really convinced him that Count S existed, and how much he even really cared about the truth.

By the way, last night Dad had wanted to pursue legal action against CELEBSTALKER19, but I was able to convince him he'd be risking exposing me and I'd never be able to show my face in school again. Fortunately, it looked like he was going to let the whole thing drop.

In any case, Count S had "left the building," and some might say he'd gone out with a whimper, by doing nothing more than charming a schoolgirl. If he'd absconded with the girl and whisked her to Paris or coaxed her into giving up her virginity, he might have had some kind of staying power. But for now, at least, Count S was milquetoast.

As for the reference to Spencer in my interview, I'd had that idea sometime in the middle of the night, too. I figured most kids would be checking the blog first thing this morning before school. Here was my opportunity to let him know nothing had happened between me and Count S, and that I was sorry.

Now it was time to get ready for school and suck whatever fame I could out of this last day of my celebrity. Mostly I was just wondering what would happen when I saw Spencer.

"Happy birthday!" Mom erupted as I scuffled from my room in my pajamas and frog slippers (don't ask). *Holy crap!* My sixteenth birthday and I had completely forgotten. I wondered if Sam had, too.

"Happy birthday, Sophie!" Kimmy greeted me along with the girls who had followed me from the school bus to schoolyard. She threw her arms around me and gave me a hug.

"It's really your birthday?" Kitty Davis asked. "Mine's in three weeks."

"How come you didn't even mention it in the interview?" asked a freshman.

"You should have told Count S. He might have given you a gift," Kelly Moses said.

"Can you believe I forgot all about it? My mother had to remind me this morning." Sam had scored brother points for forgetting it was his birthday, too. We had both been so wrapped up in yesterday's drama. Now, in some ways, it seemed a whole new era was upon us. We were one year closer to adulthood, with plans to get our learner's permits as soon as either Mom or Dad could take us down to the Registry of Motor Vehicles. We were *sixteen*, which felt about as sweet as everyone said it would.

"Nice interview this morning," Kimmy said. She winked at me.

"Yeah, so who's this kid you actually like better than the count?" Kelly asked.

"It couldn't be anyone here," Kitty said, wrinkling her nose.

"Aren't you guys bored of my life yet?" I asked.

An answer came: "Almost." I turned around. It was Spencer.

"Hey, guys, come with me and I'll tell you more about his royal hotness. I was there, too, remember?" Kimmy took over the role of pied piper. Now it was just me and Spencer.

I knew I must look like hell, having barely slept the night before. Still, for some reason, I wasn't nervous. It was as if all that had gone on in the last six weeks had caused me to grow up a little. Or maybe I'd taken to heart some of the flattering things Kardos had said to me last night. Or maybe it was just some magical transformation that takes place on your sixteenth birthday.

"Happy birthday," Spencer said. "I didn't know. I just overheard." He seemed to be the nervous one.

"Thanks. Can you believe I actually forgot my own birthday?"

"With all that's been going on, I can believe it." He nodded back his bangs. We both looked at our toes, then started talking at the same time.

"I'm sorry I—" I said.

"I know I acted like a—" he said. We both stopped and looked at each other, then laughed.

I shook my head. "You go," I said.

"I saw your interview this morning." So he knew I liked him. I felt my face get hot. "I feel like a jerk for springing that ultimatum on you. I mean, I had no right to."

"It wasn't really an ultimatum." Though it *had* felt like one.

"I shouldn't have expected you to just drop everything," he said.

"I might have if there was any way I could."

His eyes met mine. "Really?"

I smiled and nodded.

"So, you want to go for coffee after school?" Spencer flashed his million-dollar smile.

I wasn't a big coffee drinker but I could learn. "That sounds great." I smiled.

As the first bell rang, he reached down and took my hand, then pressed his warm lips to the back of it. I gasped and looked around. Kids were staring but Spencer didn't seem to care, so I didn't, either. Goose bumps migrated up my arms and up the back of my neck. He gave my hand a squeeze and let it drop.

"How'd I do?" Spencer asked.

"Think it'll take a *lot* more practice." I winked.

Here's what they say about Geminis: that they're bright and quick-witted, and that they see the world through their intellect. They love to learn, have great imaginations, and are very expressive. They also have a dual nature and are skilled at seeing both sides of a problem. Their bad traits are that they sometimes lack concentration and fail to follow through on things (which is why I need Kimmy). And worst of all, they sometimes seem ungrateful, which was something

I could easily be accused of. I'd felt cheated over some family title when I should have just stepped back and seen all the good things I have in my life. Loving parents. Sure they're divorced, but they still care about each other. And the way I see it, Taylor is just a bonus. A tolerable twin brother. The world's best friend. Some pretty interesting family heritage. And evidently, enough of whatever it is that can attract someone like Spencer Kavanaugh.

It's kind of ironic that Sam and I were born under the sign of the twins, but obviously fitting. That Saturday, Mom threw us a birthday party at the condo and invited Dad and Taylor. It felt a little weird at first, having them all in the same room, but it got easier as the day progressed. Mom and Taylor seemed to genuinely hit it off.

For the first time since birth, Sam and I each got our own cake, a sign of our moving toward independence. Sam got the Xbox he'd been whining about for months, and Mom and Dad gave me a silver necklace with a crown charm, each point bejeweled with a sparkling stone. Dad said I would always be his princess, no matter what. (And Sam said the crown was really to remind everyone how much of a royal pain I am. *Happy birthday to you, too, brother.*) The following week, we both got our learner's permits and I sort of pity our parents now, because our lives have not been the same since, with Sam and me constantly vying for time behind the wheel, and our parents growing grayer with each outing. I think I'm a better driver than Sam. He drives like a grandma. I'm just saying.

So now to the good stuff. A couple of weeks after our birthday, Dad asked Taylor to marry him and she said yes. They're planning a small ceremony on Cape Cod, at the end of the summer, in a house on the water owned by some professor friend of Dad's. Not exactly a reception for five hundred at the *Hôtel des Invalides*, but a step up from the county courthouse. I think it will be nice. Dad invited Mom and she's planning to go (and threatening to bring a date, a marketing guy named Rocko who smokes smelly cigars, but that's a whole other story, trust me). Sam finally mustered the courage to ask Michelle Alberghetti to the wedding, and to all of our amazement, she accepted. And of course Kimmy will be there, too. And maybe even Spencer.

But here's the kicker. With only a couple of weeks to go before the wedding, last night Dad sat Sam and me down in the living room again, just like that first time. Only this time Taylor was there instead of Mom.

"You sure you want to do this again?" I asked, a little irritated. I had just come home from swimming at the town pool and my wet bathing suit was starting to give me a rash. I peeled the leg elastic from the groove it had carved into my flesh.

"I have something to tell you," Dad said. "It's about the family."

"Oh boy," Sam said. "Here we go." Sam, who had just returned from his trip to Montreal before I'd ever had the chance to miss him, had been outside mowing the lawn. I could smell him from the other side of the room.

Calvo scratched at the front door. Taylor got up to let him in.

"Now, Sophie, I don't want this to upset you too much . . . ," Dad started. Once again, he seemed nervous.

"Really? Something *else* that's going to upset me? Can't anything ever upset Sam?" I asked.

"You recall our last conversation about the family titles," he said.

"Not at all, could you please go over it again?" Sam said. His sneakers were covered in grass cuttings.

"That's cold." I shook my head.

Dad ignored us and continued. "I told you how the title of countess isn't passed down to the next generation."

"Yes, I vaguely recall something about that," I said.

"What I didn't tell you at the time . . ." Dad paused. He cleared his throat. ". . . is that the title of countess is actually conferred upon *marriage* to a count."

It took me a second to process this new information. Then I turned to Taylor, who was sitting on the sofa in lotus position, breathing rhythmically. Her eyes were closed.

"Taylor gets to be the countess?" Sam asked. "What a riot!"

"Some sensitivity here, please," Dad scolded.

I felt my mouth gaping. I still hadn't found my words. Taylor's eyes blinked open. She met my gaze. Taylor was going to get to be the countess. Not me. Finally, I said, "But I'm confused. What about Mom? How come *she*—"

"Your mother chose not to take my last name, which is obviously one of the conditions. Taylor has decided to become a Delorme." Dad added, "I think she's marrying me for more reasons than just the title, though I'm not entirely sure what they are." He winked, grabbed Taylor's hand, and gave it a squeeze in another of the public displays of affection between them that had become nauseatingly frequent.

"Countess Taylor Delorme. Has a nice ring to it," she said. "But you guys only have to call me Countess in public. The rest of the time, Taylor is fine." She smiled. "And I'll only wear my tiara to breakfast."

What could I do but laugh? At that instant, Calvo jumped up on the couch and nestled into Taylor's lap. Well, if someone was going to get the title, I was glad it was Taylor.

I hadn't posted another blog entry since the day after my date with Count S. Frankly, I'd been too busy living my life, finishing up my sophomore year, and of course, tutoring Spencer every chance I got. (And yes, he did pass French.) Once school let out, I began working at the snack stand at the town pool and going out with Spencer most nights. By summer, my life had finally become interesting. But now this news of Taylor's nabbing the title of countess inspired me to make one final post, just for posterity, and because I'd been waiting for some way to gracefully wrap things up that would be sufficiently grand and satisfying to the people who'd been faithful followers. At last, I had my inspiration. By the way, I think I'm pretty good at this writing stuff. Who knows? One day you may see my name on a book cover.

> Dear friends, forgive my long silence but I've been
> otherwise engaged, quite literally, to none other than S
> himself.
>
> You see, my motives for starting this blog were those of a
> woman scorned, Count S and I having been sweethearts
> at the lycée. When he moved on, I took it upon myself to
> shine a spotlight on his antics—anonymously, of course.
> When he found out who was behind it all, his wrath

and passion were at once ignited and, well, the rest is unprintable.

Be happy for me, *mes amis*. I love you all. *À bientôt!*

Adoringly, the future Countess S